Max Gleboff

Foothold For A Loner

Prologue

"Report to my office." Major Weber's voice resounded in the radio communicator of Lieutenant Alexey Egoroff, who was training with his group at the firing range simulator. The new missile system, Storm-M, had just been deployed, but they were still trying to master these new weapons during the downtime between military operations, and so they continued to go on missions with the usual guns.

"Yes, Sir, in five minutes. I'm at the shooting range," replied Alexey, breaking off the training exercise with regret. "Continue without me. Ivan, you're in charge. Practice shooting at lightly armored targets a few more times. When I return we'll continue training how to fight in settled areas."

"Yes, we'll do that, Commander," answered Ivan without any additional questions.

Major Weber's headquarters was located about 100 meters from the bunker dug into the earth. While Alexey was on his way he had enough time to decide that it was necessary to remind the Major that his group was no longer complete. Sergeant Trenton had been wounded during a previous operation; hence, their team had lost one of its most skilled universal commandos. That was common.

As a rule, casualty rates were highest among these top paratroopers because they often had to cover their group's retreat in extreme situations. It was truly a miracle that Trenton, even though wounded, had managed to lead the adversary on a wild goose chase. More than that, he outran his pursuers and reached the meeting point. Usually, tricks like that didn't work, but still, it was clear that he wouldn't soon return to the game.

The Major's office door was open.

"Permission to enter, Major?" asked Alexey while appearing in the doorway.

"Come in and close the door. New orders just came through. Sit down." The Major touched his finger to the screen of his tablet and over the table appeared a holographic map of some semi-desert region with sandy hills, rather shallow ravines and couple of small and partly ruined buildings.

"This is the western edge of the New Wasteland. No Man's Land: 350 kilometers from the area under our control. Our recon fly-car was shot down there. It was carrying our guys on their way back from a successful raid. Presumably, it was a quarg interceptor that shot down the fly-car. We can only presume this since there's been practically no communication. A part of the group managed to survive, however. At least, we got their signal. They're somewhere here now," said the Major, highlighting in red the region of forthcoming searches on the map.

"We got to retrieve our recon men. They found something very important there. Since this isn't a standard rescue operation two interceptors will accompany you. You start in 20 minutes. Is the mission clear?"

"Yes, Major, Sir! But I'd like to remind you that I'm undermanned and of our two highly skilled universal commandos we currently only have one. Trenton was wounded; he's in the hospital and it looks like for a long time."

"I remember, but it's not that easy to find a qualified professional in this neck of the woods. However, I've got a man for this mission, but I don't know if you'll be happy. His fly-car arrives in several minutes."

"But, Major, Sir, how can I take a totally unknown fighting man on a mission? Without a sense of unit cohesion, and without getting him acquainted with the details he'll be a burden even if well-trained. And that remains to be seen."

"You don't think I know that? But the colonel wouldn't listen. He just made a reference to orders from the top and said to follow it. This means you'll have to sort things out. Flying time is about 40 minutes, enough to get a closer look at the cadet and clarify his combat role. I'll transfer his file to your tablet.

"A cadet? Is this a joke, Major, Sir?"

"Not at all, Lieutenant, it's an order. Do I have to put it in writing? The cadet is seconded to your group for one mission. Probably for two or three, depending on the results. That's all. Carry out the order, Lieutenant!"

"Yes, Major, Sir!"

Alexey left the headquarters confused and shocked. One can expect some pretty appalling things from the top brass, but this time… A cadet! Had it ever happened before: a cadet in a special forces team sent on a mission to No Man's Land? Do they want him to be killed? And the entire group as well?

Despite these grim thoughts, Alexey followed the standard mission preparation plan: let the guys know the time and place for the group gathering, as well as the requirements for gear and equipment. Next, he was going to get his own equipment, but then someone called out.

"Lieutenant, Sir, may I address you?"

Alexey turned around. He was approached by a tall and very young guy in a cadet's uniform on whose sleeve was only one single bar, to Alexey's dismay. The cadet! Nevertheless, he stopped and turned to face the man approaching him.

"Go ahead."

"Lieutenant, Sir. Cadet Igor Lavroff reporting as ordered."

Alexey looked his new subordinate over more attentively and understood that the surprises were just beginning today. The first thing that caught his eye was a holster with a Grot automatic handgun; that was quite a rare model and certainly not for cadets. Then he looked at the cadet's military decorations. Beside the emblem of the Planetary Commando Academy there were Expert and Unique Specialist badges. That didn't at all fit into the usual pattern. These two badges were rarely awarded and Alexey had never even seen junior officers with them.

The Expert badge was, as a rule, awarded to a unit commander who had secured a victory against the worst possible odds in a major battle. What on earth could a cadet do to be awarded this – that was clearly beyond all imagination. The Unique Specialist badge signified that the person possessed some very important and rare skill that allowed him to earn a victory for at least a regiment, or even for a division. Just what kind of battle was this so that the division's victory depended upon a cadet's fighting ability?

Alexey looked to the left side of the cadet's jacket which had a qualification tab. The stripe designating the cadet's theoretical background was gleaming green just a little more than one third of its length, which was only to be expected from a freshman. It should gleam in its entirety so the cadet could become an officer. The stripe designating combat experience as a soldier and /or sergeant was also necessary to become an officer; it was black, which didn't surprise Alexey at all. That meant this guy hadn't served in the army before entering the Academy, and as a rule freshmen are not sent into battle. But this freshman appeared to have officer's combat experience in abundance.

His score was more than 16,000 while the usual one for a graduate was around 100. And that was five times as much as Alexey had himself. This could only raise questions. Besides, the cadet had battle experience in senior command positions that was absolutely unexplainable. So it seemed that the cadet had fought a lot and successfully, but all the time performing officers' duties! It became clear that's how he managed to get this gun. With an Expert badge one had a right to choose his own weapons and equipment. Though, it was the same with the Unique Specialist badge. And that badge meant a lot of other nice perks as well. But going on a mission with a gun, even with one like this, was kind of…

"Cadet, is it all you have for a weapon?" Alexey glanced at the holster.

"No, Lieutenant, Sir. Most of my equipment is in my fly-car. "

That was one more peculiarity. Cadets, even the best, are not supposed to have individual fly-cars. But this was insignificant when compared with the rest.

"Well, Cadet, time marches onward. Take your things and go to the tarmac, third sector, in ten minutes. Don't get into the landing ship. Wait for me. I'll introduce you to the group. While on board we'll discuss everything in detail and check your gear. Welcome to my detachment."

"Thank you, Lieutenant, Sir. May I have permission to go?"

"Yes, go."

The Cadet quickly left for the tarmac, and Alexey hurried to get ready. Now he had even more unanswered questions. Who the hell is this guy who doesn't have to abide by the usual introduction procedure of a novice to the team? Moreover, a cadet. And yet, he is very advanced judging by his military decorations and experience. That's nonsense! One can't do that - even a very, very tough cadet. Stop. Enough. I'm gonna have to read his file. But when? Not now, that's for sure.

When Alexey reached the tarmac's third sector Lavroff was waiting for him. And he looked rather unusual. To begin with he had chosen a very exotic modification of the Storm complex to be his primary weapon. Normally, Storm was intended for heavy infantry. It was very heavy, and to use it effectively required an enhanced exoskeleton that was part of a heavy infantry rig and combined with strong armor. But this huge mass restricted mobility and shortened the combat time while using a standard battery. This is why Alexey's guys, for whom secrecy and mobility played a crucial role, had never even thought about using it.

The Cadet, however, clearly understood that so much mass will negatively effect his mobility, which is why all his exoskeleton's armor plates with heavy infantry gear were replaced by light composite protection. This allowed to reduce the overall mass and dimensions to the extent that you could install a second battery pack and an additional box for ammo. That didn't seem to be superfluous because the Storm, which includes a 30 mm automatic gun, long-barreled sniper rifle and a rotary machine-gun, had a great appetite for ammo. At the same time, the exoskeleton's lifting capacity was large enough to provide good mobility.

After carefully watching his team's new member for a while, Alexey said to the
Cadet with a tint of doubt in his voice:

"Well, move around a bit. Jump, show me a change of positions."

"Yes, Sir," answered Lavroff, jumping up three meters almost instantly. Having hit the ground he rolled 20 meters to the left, and he was almost immediately under the technical service car, pointing the barrel of his automatic weapon toward an imagined enemy.

"Hmmm, that's enough." Alexey's voice sounded neutral, but any of his team's older members understood that the Lieutenant at least wasn't disappointed by what he'd just seen. "We'll see how that's gonna look in real combat. Let's get on board."

When Alexey and his new subordinate ascended the dropship's ramp into the drop bay, the rest of the team was already there. Having glanced at the novice, they turned their puzzled gazes to their commanding officer.

"This is Cadet Igor Lavroff, who is replacing Trenton," Alexey calmly informed his soldiers, immediately spotting the bewilderment and confusion on their faces. Ivan, who was senior in rank only after Alexey, expressed what all of them felt:

"A cadet? Did we hear that right, commander?"

"You heard it right."

"But…"

"We got an order and can't discuss it. Lavroff is going with us."

"Yes, Lieutenant, Sir." Ivan's answer sounded extremely formal, which made it perfectly clear that the members of the group still didn't understand how that could be possible. "Let me ask a question, Sir."

"No, Ivan. I see all your questions written on your face and I don't have any answers. We must take off. I'll introduce him once we get under way. Cadet, take your place opposite the sergeant," said Alexey, nodding towards Ivan.

Literally a minute later the ramp went up, and the turbines started buzzing. The dropship took off from the tarmac and set a course for the destination. The escorting interceptors caught up with the ship almost immediately.

"So, Cadet, across from you is Sergeant Ivan Kelt. Deputy commander and pathfinder. To Ivan's right is Private First Class John Zeit, sniper. Next, Private Anton Gnezdoff, a universal commando and your colleague. On my right is Private First Class Kay Shefferson, communications and equipment specialist. And, finally, Private First Class Ilia

Kopytoff, physician. Now, about our mission. There's already a map on your tablets with our destination indicated.

The border of the search area is marked red. A fly-car with our long-range recon patrol was shot down there. We have to find the survivors, provide necessary assistance and evacuate them. Just as usual, we'll disembark, comb the area thoroughly, find our guys, grab them and get out of there. The meeting point to board the dropship is on the opposite border of the search area. Any questions?"

"May I speak, Commander?"

"I'm listening, Anton."

"Who will be the hen to fuss over this chick of a cadet? With his crazy outfit and his cannons he'll give us away and slow us down. Besides, he doesn't know our code signals and tactics. We'd have to give him a lot of extra voice commands, and you know how that goes with our communication systems."

Alexey looked at Lavroff, at how he'd react. But the cadet sat perfectly still and waited for the Lieutenant to answer. He was clearly interested to hear the answer despite the sarcastic question. Alexey rubbed his chin and looked at Anton.

"I've already told Ivan that I've got no answers to many questions. We'll show our code signals to the cadet now, and as for the danger of giving us away we'll find that out only on site. I hope Lavroff won't need any special care."

"Where did he get this equipment from? Who chose it for him? It doesn't fit in well with the bulk of our equipment," asked Shefferson.

"Cadet, explain," said Alexey.

"Yes, Lieutenant, Sir. I chose and prepared this equipment myself. Since I didn't have the chance to match it with the group's armaments I assumed it has to meet the basic task of a universal commando, namely to provide fire support for the group and, if necessary, provide cover for a withdrawal. Besides, I focused on the probability of acting alone, hence I maximized mobility, ammunition and power availability at the expense of protection."

"You did it yourself? Who trusted you with this? What about camouflage? You've got a huge 'barn' with cannons. How are you going to move discreetly?"

"Unfortunately, camouflage only protects from visual detection. And so I had to give it up, as I did with my protection system. But my gear is well protected from electronic surveillance equipment: there's a special scattering layer on the armor and a built-in electronic warfare device with an additional noise and decoy generator that can be adjusted so it won't bother our guys."

"Stop!" Lieutenant raised his arm in order to prevent new questions. "We don't have time. We must brief Lavroff on our group's tactics. Look here, cadet, and try to remember everything the first time I say it…"

***

Trouble started the moment they entered the No Man's Zone. The escorting interceptor that had flown ahead to do recon disappeared from the scanners. Generally, there was nothing unusual in that. The electronic warfare systems used by both sides in the conflict were much more advanced than the communication equipment, and so both faced awful communications. The interceptor, however, didn't return at the appointed time. Still, the group had its orders, and their ship continued towards the missing plane's last known location.

And this is where the enemy hit them.

The interceptor had been attacked by a ground-to-air missile - the dropship pilot's voice could be heard in Alexey's helmet. The Lieutenant noticed the interceptor make a sharp evasive anti-missile maneuver, but then it disappeared out of sight. There was no sound of an explosion.

"He evaded it," said the pilot. "He's lucky. Stop! One more missile. And one more…"

A siren's scream let the group know that their dropship was also under attack. The large and slow aircraft, unlike the interceptor, couldn't evade a missile, and the interceptor couldn't help because that pilot had his own problems.

The dropship's pilot shot off a bunch of thermal and radio-location decoys, and directed his sluggish craft downward. But the missile didn't fall for the trick. The siren continued to scream, and on top of that was the loud clanking of the ramp going down and the noise of incoming air.

"Jump, Lieutenant!" the pilot was almost shouting. "A ground-to-air missile is gonna hit us in about 20 seconds."

Alexey saw the missile coming from the back; its contrail clearly visible in the opening above the ramp that was drawn down. The missile's nose could already be seen. It approached steadily despite the decoys and the anti-missile system. Alexey understood they weren't going to make it and jumping from that height would be suicide. But then something heavy struck him on his helmet and he couldn't even see straight. He noticed it was the Cadet's armored elbow, and then a wild roar filled the compartment. The buzzing of the rotary machine-gun was unbearable, even with a helmet on, though Alexey didn't have time to pull down his visor. This hellish sound continued for just under a second. Then it all went quiet except the rattling of hundreds of cartridge cases rolling around the bay floor. Alexey heard them as if through a layer of cotton wool. The siren ceased and the ramp started closing. The dropship descended at full speed.

"Lieutenant, Sir," the pilot was still in shock, his voice trembling, "Your soldier brought down the missile. That's impossible, but he did it. We're making an emergency landing. The interceptor wasn't so lucky: he had almost evaded the missile when it was blown up remotely, and pieces from it hit his plane and the pilot had to return to base. It remains to be seen if he can do so."

Alexey's gaze focused on the cadet who had fired while on his knee and now he was getting up to return to his seat.

"How did you do it, Cadet?" Ivan's voice sounded more firmly than their ship's pilot, and it seemed he had been in similar situations more than once. Alexey always liked his calm self-restraint, and he turned to the Cadet again, concerned with the answer no less than the Sergeant.

Lavroff sat down on his seat, secured his equipment, which was obviously not superfluous before the emergency landing as Alexey remarked to himself. Then he raised his helmet visor, which had been pulled down in time, and explained:

"My helmet's data processing system has a special co-processor for calculation of deflection that's used while firing on quick moving targets, and it's interfaced with the visual recognition system. Then it's connected to the exoskeleton's pseudo muscular system that helps to aim the machine gun or the cannon. I just took up a position for shooting, identified the target, chose the weapon and pointed the machine gun at the missile. The equipment did the rest."

"Have never heard about gear like that before…" began Shefferson, but he had no time to finish his sentence. The dropship touched down and it shook. There was no time for talking. The ramp went down abruptly and the landing started.

Chapter 1

Long before that…

"So, Colonel, how do you feel?" there was clearly tension in General Clay's voice.

"Just the same for now, General, Sir," I smiled joylessly. "The doctor thinks there's a bit more than one month of normal life left for me. Then my brain will start deteriorating at an increasing rate. As far as I understand nothing can be done."

"Hmmm," the General clearly struggled for words, but then gave up and sat down on the bed's edge. "Let's put aside ranks. You're right, Dean. They don't know what to do. This is a new weapon. The enemy used it for the first time. Those who were at the epicenter saw their brains fried and fail immediately, and irreversibly. Your troop carrier just nicked the edge. At first, no one had any symptoms at all, some light-headedness at the most, but..."

"Clay," addressing the General without ranks felt more appropriate. "I've got a request..."

"Go ahead. I can deal with it."

"I'll be fine for one more month. I saw the guys from the Hawk while I was on the rescue operation after the attack. I know what awaits me. I don't want to die slowly in a hospital like a vegetable. I'm not just a planetary commando. I've got experience commanding a squad of assault robots. A major counter-offensive was launched in the 17th sector. Let me land with the first wave of commandos on one of the planets occupied by the toads. I won't be able to command any human, that's understood, and I'd never ask men to follow me to certain death. But to lead ten autonomous assault robots and to rage one last time – that's another story. A warrior with no fear of death can save many soldiers."

My words got the general thinking. The look on his face didn't change, but there was a gleam of understanding in his eyes and, as it seemed to me, approval.

"Fair enough. Although your case is unusual. I'm not 100 percent sure, but I'll do my best to make it happen."

***

For three days I was left alone except for the standard daily check-ups and medical procedures that were unavoidable for patients at the hospital. Doctors averted their eyes from me, and so everything became quite clear. On the fourth day the General came again.

"Get dressed. Quit warming up your ass here," the harsh words were an attempt to cover the awkwardness that Clay felt. "There's no point for a brigadier general to hang around here in the rear ward when his army has been assaulting Delta Kirsani for the second day already."

"I don't understand," I looked at the General raising my eyebrow.

"Ain't nothing difficult to understand. For the recent operation you've been promoted to brigadier general earlier than planned. My congratulations, Sir. At the same time your new insignia is an extra headache for me. Your request has been considered in Fleet Headquarters. The Imperial Technological Consortium has just delivered 10 brand-new assault robots to the Armed Forces. They have to face testing under the most difficult conditions. This task was entrusted to you by headquarters. I had to rack my brains on how to appoint a brigadier general to a lieutenant's post and not to seem as if I was fucking with the brains of all the captains, majors and colonels who will be your immediate supervisors."

"So, you managed to do it, General, Sir?" I gave him a little smile.

"What else was I supposed to do? Here's the deal: you and your robots will form a strike platoon reporting directly to me as before. These assault robots are new and a secret weapon, so they're not to be tested on the level of a battalion or even a regiment. I'll wait for you at the flyers' lot near the main entrance. The hospital staff has been notified. Your new uniform will be brought here."

I won't say that I was very happy to know what lay ahead, but I was relieved. After all, death in battle – that's honorable for a soldier, as well as for a general. It's much better than dying in a hospital, slobbering and wetting one's bed.

***

Nevertheless, I couldn't get everything done without messing with the minds of some officers. When I arrived to take command of my strike platoon I saw that the assault robots, which were still in their shipment packaging, were stored in a separate hangar under the guard of two boarding robots. I had to ask the technicians for assistance. Despite my rank those in charge of the logistic base clearly had enough of their own concerns, and had no time to bow and scrape before a visiting general, who with all due respect, is neither their commander nor inspector. I had a job to do, so I tended to it myself. The head of the local technical service, who appeared to be an elderly major, was extremely surprised to see a commando general at his office. Rather amused by the situation and keeping a straight face, I was the first to salute the major who came towards me from behind his desk.

"Major, Sir, this is Brigadier General Dean reporting. I arrived to get 10 Quantum-C assault robots and a small Cuirassier troop transport. I need your assistance to make the machines combat-ready."

"Eh... General, Sir." The head of technical service was clearly dumbfounded. "Why have you come in person? You'd be better off sending the robots' pilot, and we'd give him everything as best as we could. Or his company commander could come in case of the need for a special inspection."

"I'm the pilot, Major."

"You? Eh… I beg your pardon, General, Sir, that's probably not my business, but it's very unusual. In my many years I've never seen a brigadier general in command of a platoon of assault robots… Not even a colonel, not to sound too…"

"Just relax, Major. There's a first time for everything," I smiled. "Just get them prepared, and I won't inconvenience you any more with my presence."

"We'll do that in a jiffy, rest assured, General, Sir. Probably four hours, tops. I've already called the guys to the 16th hangar. I'll oversee everything personally."

"I have no doubt, Major. No doubt."

Delta Kirsani greeted me with the commotion following a major battle that had ended. The toads had dug in very well here. Everybody calls them 'toads'. Our enemies have another name, an official one, but after seeing these oversized frogs at least once you could only call them 'toads.' They're just toads.

Within a year after our fleet had left this binary star system the toads gained a foothold on all three planets that supported life, deployed orbital defense systems and built many bases within the asteroid belt. That's not to mention numerous minefields and automatic gun-missile platforms at the most strategic directions. Also, a fleet was stationed here. How could they manage without it? Orbital fortresses alone can't provide flexibility for a proper defense.

Our side took this matter seriously, and I can't even imagine how many star systems were deprived of additional forces in order to build this invasion armada. No less than 10 aircraft carriers, 14 battleships, nearly 100 cruisers, as well as a host of destroyers and corvettes. All this power came pounding down on the toads, and after busting through the mines and pilotless battle stations they hit the orbital fortresses over the fourth planet. No orbital defense could withstand such an assault. The toads' mobile forces did their best to hold onto their battle positions above the planet, plugging holes created by destroyed fortresses, but that didn't last long. Once our fleet had finished off the enemy orbiting the system's main planet, it proceeded to the neighboring planets and by now there were no enemies left in the space.

That was a glorious victory but a very bloody and costly one. You couldn't look at the victorious ships without choking up: pierced boards, gun turrets crushed by enormous explosions, gnarled and twisted flight decks. And these were the survivors – less than a half of the forces had arrived here. The toads are able to fight hard even outmatched, even when caught unawares...

Well, the orbital defense had been neutralized. It was now up to the commandos.

I piloted the Cuirassier myself. Essentially, this small troop transport was designed to be steered by the pilot of assault robots aboard. The Cuirassier was created for intersystem flights and for landing troops directly on a planet surface under favorable conditions. It can't make a hyper-jump, so I arrived to this system on the outer hangar of a large troop carrier that transported heavy assault tanks. Its captain wasn't at all happy to make a center-of-gravity recalculation before the jump and nearly told me to bug off, but then he compared his shoulder straps to those of the ballsy Cuirassier pilot and refrained from any objections.

After emerging from hyper-jump I reported to General Clay about my arrival. The first wave of commandos had already left for the fourth planet, and General Clay was too busy to say the least, but he nevertheless found the time and showed me the waiting area. The guys were clearing a foothold for a heavy equipment landing and the General ordered to be ready to join the commandos in an hour or two.

That landing order came earlier than I expected. Besides the coordinates for the landing point and short notification of safe passage, there was also Clay's comment: "Don't you dare launch any suicidal attacks. Remember the mission. You may sacrifice all your robots but give them a chance to fight well, and so that your module has a chance to send a report to the Technological Consortium".

In general, I understood that. When translated into normal language it means the following: "Don't hurry your journey to the afterlife. I still need you here, at least until the mission ends. Or almost to the end."

The landing passed without any surprises. When I landed on the surface I saw the price that the first wave paid to provide me with a smooth landing. The landing point was already cleared, but as far as the eye could see the entire area was covered with fragments of fighting vehicles, still emitting smoke. Many of the toads' tanks were still burning, but then things got really hard for us. If things continued like this then the first wave would be drained in a couple of hours.

There was a loud rumble of powerful planetary engines. The first carriers with troops and equipment started their final approach.

On the second day I realized that we were really bogged down. Our troops couldn't expand their foothold no matter how hard they tried. The toads unhesitatingly continued to send new forces into combat that had been hiding in well-disguised underground shelters. I managed to help stop an enemy tank breakthrough and beat back an airstrike of atmospheric attack planes. The hotshots from the Imperial Technological Consortium clearly knew their stuff.

My assault robots acted above and beyond my expectations, compared to the previous models. I only coordinated their actions while sitting in my heavily armored command module that was really a walking tank similar to my robots but almost twice as massive. My robots did a fine job with aerial targets. Flaming debris from three toad assault planes fell to the ground battered by explosions. The remaining two planes that sustained damage couldn't provide precision fire and hurriedly retreated by hedgehopping over the nearby forest.

It was worse with the tanks. They had strong armor, as well as force shields. An assault robot is not supposed to fight tanks head-on along flat land. They're more suitable for battle in difficult terrain, in tight conditions when it's possible to sneak up on the enemy and go for the jugular. Nevertheless, my tiny 'roaches' managed to incinerate two tanks. But they paid a great price to achieve that.

No matter what, however, tank cannon is a really a wicked thing. A robot can't survive a direct hit, and it just obliterates. Only seven of my ten robots were left, and two needed repairs. They stumbled: their scanning and navigating systems were damaged. Again I said a mental 'Thank you' to the development engineers for their great work. As soon as my robots were united in one battle network the damaged ones were given targets by their serviceable neighbors.

Soon, we realized that these adventures were just a prelude, a kind of delicacy to whet the appetite before the main course that the toads were going to serve without any delay. The toads waited until the main bulk of their troops had landed and then launched the operation. They hit us from where we didn't expect it.

Terrestrial batteries with anti-orbital cannons were always considered to be desperate weaponry, a kind of last trump card to stop attacks on troops and infrastructure from enemy ships hovering over a planet. But this time the toads demonstrated that quantity can morph into quality.

From under the surface bluster cannons appeared, mushrooming like after the rain. Well camouflaged, they previously went undetected. Hundreds of lightning strikes darted into the sky, annihilating ten troop carriers that were starting their final approach using corridors considered to be secure. Our orbital group was completely shocked, and orbital support suffered a major setback. Atmospheric planes had to stop their flights. When our battleships, with their long-range cannons, moved closer in order to neutralize the terrestrial batteries the toads counterattacked. Everyone was really shocked and depressed.

But I had asked to be here for this very moment, and it was time to do my job. I indicated the motion vector to my tiny roaches and we briskly ran to the nearest enemy battery that had just appeared out of the ground.

Quickly it became clear that I had overplayed my hand. The toads today were throwing out unpleasant surprises, one after another. As soon as the anti-orbital cannons arrived they sent out a swarm of atmospheric destroyers and attack planes. Until that moment the toads spared these swift but vulnerable machines, trying hard to shield them from orbital attack, but now it was time to use them.

The battle quickly fell into separate sectors where isolated ground units tried to fight off the air forces pressing down hard. In some places it worked pretty well, but there were too many in the sky. My assault robots started to run low on ammo. Plasma guns – that's good, but to obliterate an enemy by a guided missile is much more pleasant: the distance is greater and target accuracy is better. Only a few missiles were left, however. Two previously damaged robots were finished off rather quickly, and only five remained.

As it turned out, my small problems were nothing in comparison with what was happening in space. Almost simultaneously with the toads' attack on the planet, their ships started to appear out of hyper-jump. First, there were just a few, the fastest ones, but before long their number was equal to that of the Empire's ships. By and large, those higher up in headquarters quickly became aware of the kind of cesspool our invasion fleet had fallen into.

A counteroffensive could well result in a catastrophe. The Admiralty didn't want to push the situation to the point where it would be an irreversible clusterfuck, and so the order was given for an urgent evacuation and to leave the system.

Despite all this, I wasn't going to evacuate. For me, this was almost a perfect situation. I'd be most useful by covering the evacuating troops; that's what I was going to do. I altered the task for my robots and started to move them to the landing point while shooting our way out and taking cover behind the smoldering remains of equipment.

The orbital force continued to hold. In just the last hour our ships in orbit considerably reduced the number of enemy terrestrial batteries that had harassed them so much, and now cannon fire from the cruisers and battleships pounded the wave of armored vehicles rolling toward the ring closing around the commandos. A continuous stream of carriers landed on the cleared ground behind the troops. People quickly embarked and loaded the most valuable equipment and headed back to orbit where they started to accelerate for a hyper-jump out of the Delta Kirsani system.

New robots were added to my platoon. When a considerably battered assault company was evacuated, only the pilots and their command modules were taken into the carrier. Their robots were handed over to me. There were only seven, but now I had more robots than before. I wouldn't say that these new ones were equal to those I'd lost. The previous generation of robots was far inferior to the latest developments, but I had no reason to complain. I had gotten a generous refill of ammo because they didn't need to take it with them to orbit.

Still, the toads didn't let our commandos quit the system quietly. They regrouped their ships within the system and tried to intercept the carriers accelerating for hyper-jump. Our ships naturally rushed to defend them. A battle ensued, and soon all the big ships in the system were involved. Therefore, the remaining troops on the surface couldn't rely anymore on support from orbit.

We felt the impact immediately. The insolent atmospheric planes pushed forward raining missiles down on us, as plasma poured from cannons. Enemy tanks started a new attack, pushing aside the debris of equipment knocked out of action. Few of us remained since the main body of troops had been evacuated. As the senior officer among those on the surface, I ordered to abandon the equipment and make a run to orbit in my Cuirassier that stood on the edge of the landing site.

They tried to make me fly with them, but I repeated with a certain pleasure some colorful figures of speech used by a sergeant at the military school where I was a cadet. All the subordinates evidently had a similar experience, so they obeyed, jumping into the Cuirassier, and with an enviable swiftness rushed into the sky.

The equipment was not just left behind but was hooked up to my command module. Thanks again to the engineers, my module was able to control this motley crew, although at first I doubted it. I now commanded almost a battalion comprised of 50 assault robots, a couple of heavy assault tanks, two launchers of short range missiles and even three armed unmanned atmospheric planes.

The toads immediately took an interest in the Cuirassier's take-off and were about to shoot, but I didn't let them. My motley crew made a frontal attack, imitating a breakthrough of the defensive ring. I told half of my robots to shoot down the missiles launched at the Cuirassier, and the rest they destroyed at point of launch.

My attack fizzled out almost at once, however, as was expected. After all, we were greatly outnumbered. In just 90 seconds both of my assault tanks were burning with smoky fire, only one-third of the assault robots remained. The launching racks were now a useless heap of junk since no one was left to reload and the ammo was gone. Atmospheric planes were shot down while covering the transport ships. Still, I bought the Cuirassier 90 seconds; they had a chance.

Generally speaking, I should have been dead by now. I was still alive, but I had no idea what to do next. I completed my mission but I couldn't be evacuated. I could go on fighting, of course, but there was no point.

I continued to direct my robots while trying to find a solution. My thoughts were interrupted by a call. We had agreed with General Clay that there would be no farewells and no ritual verbiage, hence I was caught off guard by this call. Since it was the top brass, I had to respond.

"This is Brigadier General Dean, you have my full attention," reverberated the words in an official tone in my helmet telecom system.

"Stop this fucking circus, Dean. Why the hell didn't you answer my call? Get out of there. Now!" General Clay used approximately the same words that I'd used some ten minutes prior to convince my subordinates to board the Cuirassier.

"Well, Clay," I responded tiredly, ignoring protocol. "We agreed upon everything."

"Brigadier General, when was the last time you were in solitary?! Have you forgotten how to address a senior officer?" screamed Clay, which was unusual for him, changing the subject right away. "There's a message from headquarters. Doctors demand you return, we need you intact. They've found a solution, and not only for you, but for all of us, for the whole Empire. And it's all to do with you. Exclusively! You understand? What's with your theater show?! Turn the beacon on immediately and stop trying to be a hero!"

"I have no way out. I'm completely encircled, and the toads are finishing off my robots. There's only 10 left. Fuck…," my module's force field was hit from above and was thrown about, but wasn't severely damaged.

"What happened?"

"Nothing serious, yet. Some operational issues. I turned the beacon on."

"I see. Wait. And don't you dare die. You've got it, General?"

"Yes, Sir. My mission is not to die. Do I have permission to carry it out?"

"Once you reach my ship, I'll show you!"

I didn't listen. Behind the thin chain of my robots was a small relatively vacant patch of space in front of a heap of burnt iron debris. That's to where we were slowly moving back, snapping shots at the toads' most impudent flyers and terrestrial drones. Good thing they had run out of heavy tanks, otherwise I'd quickly been screwed. There was no good news in my situation.

The medium-range scanner buzzed, and 19 small high-speed air targets appeared on the screen. That was a missile salvo. How fortunate that there was almost nothing left to deal with them. Just guns. I had run out of guided missiles seven minutes ago, and I directed my module to the enormous pile of burnt heavy machinery.

On top of this heap of wreckage our heavy tank stood with its hull side split open and the turret smashed. Hiding behind it, I sent my robots to the opposite side where they began to shoot at the approaching missiles. The toads became quiet, and didn't want to get hit by their own missiles. My robots performed very well and managed to shoot down nine missiles… Then an explosion!

The tank behind me, where I was hiding, was knocked over by a shock wave, but I managed to get out of the way. As I'd hoped the incoming missiles were aimed at targets that were actively fighting back.

"General, do you hear me?"

"Yes, Dean, I hear you well."

"I'm alone now, the robots have been blown to bits."

Before Clay could answer, a toad drone appeared, jumping on the tank that was on its side. We fired almost simultaneously at each other, the enemy was blown away from the tank and disappeared behind a heap of debris. My module's force shield repelled the intense plasma strike, but the generator burnt out from overload and only my armor could protect my vulnerable module.

"Lie down!" I heard the general shouting in my helmet's headphones.

I fulfilled the order without thinking, and I did so right in time. The area around me became a fiery inferno. The main battleship's cannons ain't no aircraft gun. I've already seen something like that… The air above me was filled with howling pieces of armor flying in all directions, as well as pieces of concrete and various debris. You don't want to get caught in the way of these projectiles. Heavy blows banged the module's armor, but lucky for me the shards couldn't pierce it.

When the dust settled I saw an approaching corvette. Usually, space warships don't enter the atmosphere, but this was clearly a very special case. The battleship above continued shooting while taking on fire from 800 meters away. Clearly there were no worthy targets left in my vicinity. I didn't wait for an invitation and rushed to the corvette as fast as I could. My module tumbled into the ship's hold while general Clay urged me on, hollering with such great skill that even the legendary sergeant from military school would have been envious.

Chapter 2

"General, Sir…"

"You can put ranks aside, Dr. Silk."

"Ehh…, yes, of course. So, Dean, have you heard anything about mental fields?" The medical colonel glanced at me questioningly.

Our conversation was informal. General Clay brought me to the Admiralty's central clinic and handed me over to the local vanguard of medical science who were going to explain everything. Clay also wanted to attend and brought along two generals whom I had caught a glimpse of before at headquarters.

"I only know that your department is working on this matter; nothing more."

"Well, I see no reason to go into detail, but there are a couple of points that I really want to make clear. Until recently the physical nature of this substance wasn't certain. Plenty of empirical data attested to the existence of mental fields and to the fact that such fields allowed for the instantaneous transfer of information from the brain activity of intelligent beings across a very large distance. At the same time, the principles of controlling these fields were, and still are, beyond our comprehension. Strangely enough, the enemy attack that you were a victim of, along with 1,500 members of our military, has led to a breakthrough. Whatever was used by the … ehh, toads, which so it seems, that's how you call them - functioned on the basis of mental fields, but it definitely used their vibrations as one of the harmful effects. In general, the details aren't important, but we've found the key to a partial understanding of this phenomenon while studying the changes in victims' brains. Bear with me a little longer,

I'm coming to the main point. We've modernized one of our experimental units and now we have a kind of scanner allowing to study the extent of mental fields at great distances from us. I'm talking about millions of light years. At lesser distances signals merge, unfortunately, and are distorted by interference, but that's secondary. The important thing is we've discovered a human civilization. It's very far from us, and we can't even indicate the precise direction. We've been lucky with this coincidence of circumstances, and we've managed to gain access to the mental field of a comatose man. He's sick. At their medical level he's terminally ill, but we know this disease and are able to cure it. Their civilization is significantly less advanced than ours - some 200 years behind, at least. They recently discovered hyper-jump and started launching interstellar flights, and almost instantly they bumped into a hostile race, a humanoid, but not a human one. There's a war on there, just like here. I wouldn't say they're loosing, but this war is all-consuming with apparently no end is in sight."

"And how could they help us?" this question from my mouth was clearly written on the faces of all those present who still weren't in the know.

"Generals, Sirs, tell me honestly, will we be able to win this war?"

There was a long silence in the doctor's office. Eventually, it was broken by Clay.

"This is a very difficult question, Dr. Silk. Let's say, if there won't be any great innovation in the field of armaments, we'll lose."

"And how long can we keep going? After all, we're not the only ones with possible breakthroughs in new weapons; our enemy might as well."

"The war has been going for almost 100 years. For now, we still have somewhere to retreat, but this can't last forever. We have 20 years, probably 30 if we're lucky."

"And what happens next?"

"It gets pretty grim after that, doctor. We'll be chased out of the developed worlds system interconnected by a network of stationary hyper-portals, and we'll have nowhere to go except intergalactic space. But I don't think they'll let us go. They'll catch up and destroy us. The toads can manage hyper-jumps as well as we do."

"Here's an answer to your question. We need a place to run to in case things turn out bad. You have this place. We found it for you."

"But how do you expect to get there? You can't even point in the right direction. Even if you knew it, what's the point? A linear motion that far in hyperspace will take thousands of years. What we need is a stationary portal, a couple of gates at our side and theirs. Besides, we must know the exit's subspace coordinates."

"That's why you plucked our heroic Brigadier General out of that mess in Delta Kirsani. The thing is that the General's brain was exposed to radiation from the toads' artifact and has been altered. Now it can harmoniously resonate with the brain of a young man lying in a coma millions of light-years away, and that means we can transfer General Dean's mind into that man's brain. Moreover, we can download much knowledge into it, and that can be of immense service to the general when he's there."

"Excuse me, doctor," I was amazed. "But I wasn't the only man exposed to radiation. You've got at least a thousand patients like me at your hospitals."

"We've examined all of them. Unfortunately, they're not suitable because of the individual peculiarities of their brains. We're lucky to have you. Your experience will be extremely helpful there."

"But that man is incurably sick and in a coma…"

"This alone has enabled us to connect to his brain. Coma and his disease – these are undoubtedly problems, but there is a solution. While transferring your senses we'll download an enormous amount of information into your brain, including the means of treating this disease. Your brain won't make it, however. If it had been possible to instruct everyone in this manner then we'd have defeated the toads long ago. Alas, a human brain can't bear a direct data download. Your case, however, is very special. Your brain will die, but it won't matter. Your senses, including the downloaded information, will be transferred into a new body."

"And what if I die while still in a coma?"

"It's highly unlikely. Transfer of senses stimulates brain activity and the immune system of the recipient. You will almost certainly have two or three weeks of remission. Within this period of time you'll have to solve the problem."

"After that you've got a military career ahead of you, general," said General Filt, the highest-ranking officer among those present. "You're used to it. You'll have to strive to a high position in the power structures of our potential allies and provide for the construction of the second gate of a stationary hyper-portal. Your brain will hold all the necessary knowledge and hyper-coordinates. And we'll construct our gate here. We've already found a god-forsaken place on the periphery of the galaxy for the gate, and if things turn bad we'll still have a chance to survive as a species and to start all over again."

"And what about that civilization? They may be reluctant to accept us."

"That'll depend on you in many ways, General. Actually, there's much common ground between us. Both of us are humans, hence, we'll be able to come to an understanding. We'll provide technological advances and help them to win the war. They'll help us develop new territories for our settlements or invite us to their planets if they wish. Anyway, we won't impose ourselves. In case they don't want to collaborate we'll go into unexplored space and start all over again.

"Dr. Silk, are you ready to do it, from the technical point of view?" I was highly excited and couldn't control my feelings.

"Practically, yes. We have to do a little fine-tuning of the equipment, and that's not possible without your participation. What we need is your consent."

"My consent?" I made a half-smile. "You have it."

***

Behind the open window of the nurses' room a light wind blew the poplar's twigs. It was early June and the smells of summer covered the specific hospital odor of the furniture and the walls. Olga sat in the armchair having crossed her legs, and looked through the news of the day on her tablet. Upon hearing the equipment beep she jumped up and rushed to look at the patient's monitor. Her hand automatically pushed the call button.

"What happened, Olga?" asked the doctor on duty via the communicator.

"Ilja Sergeyevich, the patient in the sixth emergency room has regained consciousness."

***

I awoke with a terrible headache; my head was hurting so much that I wanted to be unconscious again. I didn't even try to open my eyes because I knew that the light would just make things worse.

A door opened with a slight click, and someone entered the room, or maybe the ward. I made an effort and slightly opened my eyes. Despite my worst expectations the pain didn't intensify. Quite the opposite: I was lying on a narrow bed around which were cumbersome medical devices standing on tripods and supports, flashing with dozens of lights of many colors. My body was connected to these contraptions via transparent tubes and cables. Also, I was covered from head to toe with sensors, injectors and other devices that electrically stimulated the muscles, judging by the occasional light pricking that I felt.

Two people entered the ward: a middle aged man with a flat device in his arms and a young attractive woman behind him. They came towards me.

"How do you feel?" asked the man looking at me attentively.

The language he spoke seemed perfectly strange to me and sounded very unusual. Nevertheless, I understood everything he said. Dr. Silk had warned me before the transfer that both my new body's memory and skills would remain. But fluent knowledge of a foreign language leaves one with a strange feeling.

"I have a bad headache," I tried I to answer, and judging by his nod, I succeeded.

"That's not surprising, Igor. You've awaken. This is amazing. We expected it no earlier than three days after the radial therapy, and it's been only one day."

"I see, Ilya Sergeyevich," I managed to recall the doctor's name and was glad. "Can you do something for my headache so that I can think clearly."

"Yes, Igor, but it's best to sleep now. Olga, give the patient some dekateral."

"Ilya Sergeyevich," I tried to make my voice sound firm. "You know I have little time left. I prefer to spend it conscious. I've plenty of unfinished business and I want to see it all through to completion before... you know what."

The doctor knew. Asteroid fever's terminal stage leaves a man with no chance to act consciously: the pain is so strong that even powerful drugs can't help.

Ilya Sergeyevich wanted to object but he changed his mind.

"Olga, forget the dekateral. Use maltrin. Can I do something else for you, Igor?

"Yes, please. Could I ask for a tablet and network access?"

"Of course. Olga will bring everything you need."

"And...," listening to my cravings, "can I have something to eat?"

"You have an appetite? That's quite unusual. You've been fed intravenously for some time, hence your stomach isn't used to normal food. You can start with a mug of vegetable broth, no more than that. Anything else?"

"Thank you, Ilya Sergeyevich, nothing else."

After the shot of maltrin my headache receded. Nurse Olga got me a tablet and a mug of hot vegetable broth, and I tried to recall from my renewed memory all the information for the treatment of asteroid fever that Dr. Silk's brilliant guys had put in my head. We called this disease by another name. Here, miners working in the asteroid belt were the first to get this 'bug', and so the name stuck. These humans were lucky that asteroid fever posed a risk to just three percent of the population.

Due to its particular qualities the pathogenic agent couldn't survive in the bodies of the vast majority of people. If this fungus, however, found a way to survive in the hostile environment of the human body, then it began to modify cells into a favorable form. This process in the early stages was very slow since the immune system killed most of the malignant cells, but gradually the modified cells increased and their number grew steadily. They continued to divide, generating new cells that replaced the normal ones. The lesions grew in size: first a man felt a certain discomfort, then pain, and then organ failure. Eventually, it was like an avalanche and a person died in terrible agony.

Doctors tried to stop this disease, and drug treatments and radiation therapy slowed and even partially reversed the spread of the affected cells. But this treatment greatly damaged the body because the medicine was highly toxic, as was the radiation. The modified cells died, but healthy cells also were killed. As a result, in just a few months death occurred no matter what.

In my world they found a treatment for this disease 150 years ago, and it came unexpectedly at the intersection of two very different sciences: biochemistry and nuclear physics. Now my task was to convey the essence of the idea to people capable of making the necessary equipment.

All right, let's try to analyze our assets and liabilities – me and my new body. I, Igor Yakovlevich Lavroff, just 15 years of age, five feet eleven inches tall, am thin and now look like a skeleton. I'm neither handsome, nor ugly. I'm Russian, a citizen of the Earth Federation. I am a resident of Saturn's moon, Titan, in the Solar system terraformed by Russians long before all the states on Earth merged to form a single political entity. I am on Titan at the moment. I study, or rather, studied at high school, specializing in xenology. Hence, I study mankind's malicious enemies.

My father perished five years ago in the asteroid belt near the Van Maanen star system. Why the quargs were so interested in this dim white dwarf in the Pisces constellation remains unknown. However, we fought desperately for it. The fight ended in a draw, but my father never returned home. No details were given about his fate. We were just told that the merchant ship where he was head doctor had been hit by a powerful torpedo from a quarg destroyer. No one survived.

My mother taught at a local elementary school. We lived off her salary, which was decent, as well as the state compensation for my father's death. But after I fell ill our savings soon ran out. Insurance wouldn't cover all the medical bills.

Now, I have two weeks left, probably three, although I shouldn't rely on this.

Actually, that's all that was significant. I didn't really know much. I'm physically underdeveloped, not to mention this damned disease… On the other hand, all this refers to Igor Lavroff, and there is another me, Brigadier General Dean of whom nobody here knows anything. And Brigadier General Dean has an incomparable trump card in his pocket: the knowledge put in his brain. That was the card that could be and should be put on the table right now.

I sipped some hot and tasty vegetable broth from my mug, thinking about how to start. I could ask for the doctor and explain the treatment for asteroid fever, but he'll probably think I was panicking due to my fear of an imminent death. As a mere teenager, and certainly not a genius, there was no logical way I could know such things, especially since Ilya Sergeyevich knew my father. They weren't friends, but were on good terms. The doctor knew enough about me and wouldn't believe in my sudden enlightenment without solid proof.

So, I shouldn't start with him, but with independent people who are competent in the areas important for me. I need to attract their attention, must be interesting to them, and must convince them to listen carefully to me. And where should we look for them, Mr. 15-year-old Brigadier General? Well, what do we lack to be taken seriously? Education - an official confirmation of my qualifications. Hence, it was clear that I should look for such people in institutions of higher learning.

I began to surf the web. What am I interested in? Medicine in general, and biochemistry in particular. On the other hand, I need physics; can't get by without it. What do we have here on Titan? Ok, The Colonial Technological Institute. That's what I need. Well, that's for physics and probably for biochemistry. What about medicine? Oh! A branch of the Military Medical Academy. That will do! Where do we start? Physics is closest to me since my days as a general.

I found the distance learning section on the Colonial Technological Institute's website. Distance learning is encouraged and supported by the Earth Federation. It's free of charge and to start I only have to pass the admission exam. Then, at the end of each stage is another test. Well, how interesting this is: I'll be able to do all the training without meeting professors, even online. If something isn't clear, I'll be able to consult a professor online, but it's not obligatory. Besides, there are no limits regarding the time frame for completion of the curriculum. I can take exams even 10 times a day. Great! As for the mandatory course exam, it includes the grading of tests by a professor in person or a commission. In case they have questions, I must answer in person. Well, I'll make sure they have questions. Personal contact – that's what I really need.

I enrolled in the distance learning section by placing my finger on a sensor, and signed the contract using a personal digital signature. As expected, I had no problems with the admission test and I became a student.

There were concerns that the knowledge placed in my brain would in practice appear to be something like an encyclopedia, that is to say a repertoire of knowledge, no more than that. From the experience of my former life I remembered that theoretical knowledge wouldn't necessarily provide a student with the skills to solve problems or to perform practical study. To do that one needs special training and additional skills.

In case my concerns should materialize then I'd most likely face some difficulties when taking further exams that included both theoretical issues and problems to solve, as well as lab experiment imitations. But my worries proved to be in vain. All the knowledge successfully settled in my brain. I don't know if this was

Dr. Silk's accomplishment or the stimulation of my new brain by the transfer of senses properly arranged as it should be. Anyway, I understood almost immediately what had to be done while taking the exams.

The exams seemed endless: I spent about four hours continuously tapping on the tablet's virtual keyboard and answering questions aloud. Nurse Olga twice entered my room and asked if it was time to rest. I answered that I felt better, and claimed that such activity was evidently doing me good. She shook her head unbelievingly, but apparently the monitor's readings and the way I looked confirmed my words, hence she didn't object.

The final test took me two hours and it was very interesting. I enjoyed it so much that I didn't noticed a small thumbnail image that appeared in the corner of my display. That was Professor Stein who had connected with my tablet. He waited in silence until the test was over. I leaned back on my pillow satisfied, and he said:

"Good afternoon."

Quite surprised, I twitched slightly. I brought the tablet closer to my face in order to reduce the webcam's field of view and turned on a video link. The professor appeared to be in his fifties, although I could be wrong since I didn't really know what the local doctors were capable of.

"Good afternoon, professor. I'm really glad you dropped in."

Stein raised his eyebrow, clearly amazed.

"To what do I owe this pleasure?"

"You've made it possible for me to get in touch with a competent authority and to express some ideas."

"Really? But I'm here not for this. At least, for the moment. Igor Yakovlevich."

"Just call me Igor. Sorry for interrupting you, professor."

"Hmmm, well, Igor, then call me Ivan Gerkhardovich. So, Igor, you've surprised everybody here and, to be perfectly frank, instigated a number of queries and questions. I'll specify them one by one. First, you passed the admission exam with the highest mark, being just 15 years old. Well, that's not unheard of. It happens. Second, you already passed all the midterm and final exams, with the highest scores. Now, that doesn't happen. Third, you never before demonstrated such knowledge. All children prodigies participate first in children's contests, then in school competitions, win grants; in brief, they have a high level of activity in a certain area before entering high school. But you haven't proved yourself at all. You specialize in xenology. Your marks have been average, you scored four out of five in physics and you just completed the ninth grade. You shouldn't even be able to pass the admission exam."

"However, here am. Ivan Gerkhardovich, ask me questions."

"I've already asked, Igor. And if you don't understand the question, I'll briefly reiterate. How is this possible?"

I went silent, and then sighed and pushed the tablet aside so that the ward became visible in the webcam.

"I've had a very strong incentive, professor. VERY strong. I've had asteroid fever for six months. I want to stay alive, Ivan Gerkhardovich. I need your assistance."

To say that Stein was confused would be a colossal understatement. The professor just lost it.

"But... how can I help you?" he asked, pulling himself together. "I work in theoretical physics, not in medicine."

"Ivan Gerkhardovich, may I ask for a meeting in person? I'd like to describe a treatment for my disease in which nuclear physics plays an important role. I need an expert to confirm that my idea is not the ramblings of a dying man. Otherwise no one will believe me."

The professor stared at me pensively.

"Let's finish with the exam first, Igor. I'd like to see the depth of your knowledge beyond standard testing. I want to see how serious it is. Are you ready?"

"Sure I am."

"First, a math question that is decisively inseparable from theoretical physics. Are you familiar with Kanthor-Shiman's conjecture?"

"Yes. I'm familiar with Kanthor-Shiman's theorem."

"Theorem?"

"Yes, namely, a theorem. I can provide proof."

"That's unexpected. You have my attention."

"Five minutes please."

My fingers started to flutter over the virtual keyboard. The proof extracted from my memory covered one and a half standard pages. Near the end I intentionally allowed a small mistake while indicating the boundary conditions that were not totally correct. I hoped the professor would find this small mistake that would not seriously affect the course of the proof.

Stein examined the file for half an hour shaking his head in astonishment from time to time, then he looked up at me. He did everything just as I expected.

"That's great, young man, just great. But there is a mistake, it seems you may have been a bit hasty. This term - he put the part of the proof in question on the screen - should look like this. And the professor corrected my mistake."

"I totally agree with you, Ivan Gerkhardovich," I uttered gratefully. "I hadn't realized that. But you corrected me just in time. It seems to me that Kanthor-Shiman-Stein's theorem sounds much better than Kanthor-Shiman's conjecture.

I smiled and looked him in the eye.

Stein looked at me thoughtfully.

"That's wrong," he finally expressed his doubts. "Stein-Lavroff's proof will sound far better. That's more than enough to pass the exam. I'll send your diploma in 10 minutes. Congratulations on graduating from the Colonial Technological Institute."

"Thank you, professor. And what about a meeting in person?"

"I understand," Stein looked around my room, "you're inviting me to your place?

"Yes, if it's possible."

"OK. When?"

"I need to invite two more people, and I don't yet know if they will. To tell you frankly, I don't even know who are they."

"What particular areas do you need specialists from?"

"Medicine, radiotherapy, and biochemistry."

"Do you know biochemistry as well as physics?"

"I think so."

"Then I have a worthy candidate. I'll persuade him to come."

"I'll appreciate that. Is he your colleague at The Colonial Technological Institute?"

"Yes."

"I'll take the biochemistry exam tomorrow. Could you ask him to examine me?"

"Well, that's easy to arrange."

I spent the following two days on the tablet. Olga was very concerned that I'd tire myself and called on the doctor's assistance. Ilya Sergeyevich came in, greeted me and approached me silently, looking at what I was doing, which was one of the medical assignments; namely, I was conducting virtual surgery to remove shrapnel from a patient's left lung. After standing a couple of minutes behind my shoulder, the doctor silently left my room and closed the door quietly. What he thought, I don't know; but he had no questions, and Olga didn't bother me anymore.

As for biochemistry, I passed with flying colors, but with medicine I had a hard time. There are a lot of practical matters in this discipline, even with the automation of the main processes. Besides, all the medical equipment was completely unfamiliar to me. Nevertheless, I obtained all the required three diplomas, and set up a meeting with three professors. Local science was enriched by Lutsko-Lavroff's cell membrane permeability estimation method, Lavroff-Grishin's radiotherapy tolerance express test, and Stein-Lavroff's proof.

On the fourth day my 'mom' visited me. She was so glad that I felt better and I decided to tell her some things. Quite surprisingly, even though I was an orphan I saw this older but attractive woman as my mom. Igor Lavroff was a kind homeboy and loved his mother very much. A part of his personality apparently settled in my head, and having nothing against it, I wondered about that myself.

Mother sat down on a chair near my bed and took my hand in hers.

"Igor, you clearly feel better. Perhaps, everything will be fine."

"If we keep on going the way we're going, it won't be okay," I replied firmly. "This is just a remission, a temporary improvement. Within a fortnight I'll be in worse condition and it will be irreversible."

"But how… Ilya Sergeyevich told me nothing."

"And he won't. He doesn't want to ruin the last days with your son. But there is something he doesn't know, mom. Tomorrow three professors will come here to see me: a radiotherapy specialist, a biochemist and a physicist. Please come. It will be useful for you to hear our conversation. And one more thing. I'm afraid we may need all the money we have. Everything that's left."

Chapter 3

I notified Ilya Sergeyevich in advance about the professors' visit and asked him to also be present at the meeting. He looked at me somewhat strange but didn't say anything aloud: he had evidently decided that the terminally-ill patient was just grasping at a straw and he should be allowed to continue since there was no sense in making him upset before his death.

The guests arrived almost simultaneously. In any case, my doctor let them enter my ward together. My mother had already been there. She quietly said "Hello" to the scientific luminaries and sat down on a small corner sofa. I introduced my new acquaintances to her and started our conversation.

"So, gentlemen, I know you are busy people, therefore I'll get right to the point. I'd like to show you a treatment for asteroid fever that I've come up with. I'd like for you to assess it and help further develop It In order to test on me."

"So, you just came up with it out of thin air, Igor?" asked Professor Grishin.

"Not at all, Fyodor Nicolayevich, I was racking my brains thinking it over. You can't imagine how stimulating it is for mental performance when the Grim Reaper stands behind you with his scythe." I smiled, remembering that it was not the first terminal diagnosis in my life. "However, let's get to the point."

I turned my tablet so the guests could see the image of two cells on the screen.

"As you can see here, there is a healthy cell and a modified cell. Many of their properties are identical, which makes the targeted destruction of modified cells difficult. At the same time, there are some differences." I displayed on the screen the next slide with the formula of an organic matter with a rather complicated spatial structure. "This is methylfenolithyn. Its molecule is just what we need to make use of the structural differences between a healthy and a modified cell. It can't penetrate a healthy cell, but a modified cell membrane will let it pass easily."

"But Igor," Professor Lutsko cut me off. "You've just aced your biochemistry exam. Substances of this type have long been known and have been tested on numerous occasions including certain attempts to cure asteroid fever. We always face the same intractable problem: at low concentrations the active substance doesn't injure a modified cell, but if we increase the concentration then a patient dies of intoxication earlier than the modified cells die."

"You're absolutely right, professor," I nodded my head. "But we shouldn't use methylfenolithyn at high concentrations. It's marked by an ability to easily add a Boron atom without losing its ability to selectively penetrate modified cells."

"Hold on, Igor," Professor Stein stopped me. "Now I seem to understand why you need a nuclear physicist. Aren't you going to use the isotope, Boron-10, in your method?"

"You're exactly right, professor."

"Then let me continue," Stein was evidently in a state of scientific excitement. "Boron-10 has a high propensity to capture slow neutrons that trigger energetic and short-range secondary alpha particles and lithium-7 heavy ion radiation. Tell me, Fyodor Nikolayevich," Stein turned to Professor Grishin. "How does the human body respond to slow neutron radiation?"

"Well, when the exposure and dose of radiation are reasonably measured thermal neutrons just pass through the human body; they're not absorbed by human tissues and do not damage them."

"OK. Now imagine how with the help of this substance, what's its name…?"

"Methylfenolithyn," I told him.

"Yes, thank you. So, with the help of methylfenolithyn we inject Boron-10 atoms into the affected cells and expose a patient to slow neutron radiation. What happens then in the diseased cells? A tiny nuclear explosion in each, a nuclear fission of one atom. What do you think, professor," Stein addressed the biochemist. "How much energy is needed to destroy a diseased cell while keeping everything around intact."

"Let me estimate," muttered Lutsko who threw himself into the calculations with the help of his tablet. "Here it is. Two or three mega-electron volts will be enough, otherwise it will be risky."

"This is exactly the amount of energy released when a Boron-10 atom splits. I don't know what my colleagues think, but I think your method will work, Igor. In fact, our institute has a slow neutron source reactor, although it's bulky. So, if we're going to help this young genius, then we should take him to our quarters."

"Frankly, I see nothing to stand in the way of this method from the point of view of biochemistry," added Lutsko. "However, there's a certain danger for the patient due to the toxicity of cellular debris that can poison him."

"It won't," Professor Grishin and my doctor were speaking with one voice. Then Ilya Sergeyevich continued: "The detox procedures after radiation therapy are well elaborated and we have all the necessary equipment here."

"Wait, gentlemen, please," Lutsko got a word in edgewise. "We somehow got carried away. The idea certainly deserves attention. This is, fair to say, a great idea. But we are not a club of medical enthusiasts. I think you understand that many months are needed to implement the idea. There needs to be animal testing, then clinical trial. And our young colleague has only … how much time?"

"No more than a couple of weeks," I answered trying to keep a calm tone of voice.

My mother gave a kind of sob, and the whole room fell awkwardly silent.

I broke the silence: "It's a solvable problem. I'll present a detailed description of the treatment methodology and specify that I developed it myself and insist on it being tested on me; copies of my diplomas will be attached. I'll take full responsibility for any consequences. When the document specifies that I'm the methodology author, nobody can accuse you of dragging a desperate man into the test of an untried treatment. This document will have the digital signatures of both myself and my mother, and each of you will get a copy. If I die there'll be clear proof to exonerate you of negligence. If I don't, we'll just destroy these files and you'll submit patent applications to the Patent Office for Stein-Lutsko-Grishin-Golovanov's treatment for asteroid fever. Do you have an idea of the potential amount of royalties?"

"Oh, yes, we do," answered Grishin for everyone. "But you've forgotten again to mention Lavroff, as the very first."

The four of them looked at me silently.

"How much money is needed for this treatment?" I asked the question that tormented me.

The professors looked at each other. Stein rubbed the tip of his nose with his index finger and remarked in a thoughtful tone:

"You and me, each of us has a 100,000 roubles from the discretionary fund of the Colonial Technological Institute for solving Kanthor-Shiman's conjecture. Have you recently checked your personal bank account? In fact, I don't think you'll need more for this treatment, but just in case... you can also count on my share."

"And for my share," added Lutsko. "I have my earnings from Lutsko-Lavroff's method."

"And for Lavroff-Grishin's express test as well..."

"Gentlemen," my doctor nudged the professors back to the main topic in a business-like manner. "At what time should the patient be ready for transport?"

They started to discuss the details. I didn't listen and just looked at my mom, who sat silently on the corner sofa as big tears rolled down her cheek.

***

I can't say that it went smoothly. Slow neutron radiation turned out to be more harmful than expected, and my body already had so many modified cells that the results of their degradation considerably intoxicated my body. The doctors, however, brought me back from the brink, though barely. Time was needed to prepare all the necessary medicine. A couple more days and my situation would have been irreversible, but everything worked out.

While I was in the hospital in the care of Ilya Sergeyevich and Olga, I had several serious conversations with the professors, who were now my partners. They worked endlessly around the clock and were overjoyed by what was happening. They often brought eminent doctors from the Earth Federation to visit me - I was a real miracle, a terminally ill patient cured of asteroid fever. Most of all, the esteemed guests were impressed that the patient was the main patent holder.

They cautiously asked me about the treatment's details and looked very puzzled to get professional answers from a 15-year old boy who was half alive.

Each professor proposed that I do post-graduate studies and hinted about a great scientific career, but for the moment I kept silent. On one hand, I didn't plan to become a researcher; on the other hand, I didn't want to offend these nice people. In general, it was high time that I decided my further plans.

A career as a researcher might offer a promising future, but that was only at first glance. Despite the war against an external enemy that lasted for more than 20 years, the Earth Federation was an amorphous entity. In the time before the era of space exploration it had inherited divisions in a number of regions that were once independent states. While they jointly explored outer space, their colonies were very different from one another: one was populated predominantly by Russians; another by Chinese; or by Americans and Europeans; or by Arabs… All these colonies were autonomous. The threat of external aggression was the reason to unite. Humans should be thankful to the quargs for that. Nevertheless, secessionist tendencies persisted in the Earth Federation, which was understandable since it had been established by force.

Each autonomous region conducted its own scientific research and competed with one another. Thus, the Earth Federation's scientific community was highly fractured; basically, a snake pit of competing experts. With all that knowledge in my head I could accomplish a great deal in the scientific world, but I wouldn't be able to change civilization's development vector, for example, to force it to unite and to spend significant resources on research in this time of war.

The military was the only core institution that united the state. Since the war began, an entire generation of young men had grown up. For them, a peaceful life existed only in films, books and the tales of older people. They hadn't seen life without war, and couldn't imagine what it was like. No one could even predict an end to the armed confrontation between humans and quargs. Thus, there were no other possibilities for me except for a military career. Only as a high-ranking military officer could I have a significant influence in policy formulation. Well, I'll just have to become a cadet again. I was used to it.

It wasn't that easy to enter the Military Academy. Unlike other educational institutions there was no distance learning. Also, my age was a problem. Since I was just 15 I couldn't enter the Academy this year. I had to wait until next year. I was reluctant to waste my time, but after having carefully read the requirements and having looked through different forums that discussed military academies I understood that one year might not be enough to prepare.

To begin with, excellent physical fitness is required, and I was frail and weak. Though cured of my illness, a long rehabilitation period still awaited me, so I had some nine or ten months to get my feeble body into good shape.

My social origin appeared to be another problem. My father was a civilian doctor, my mother a teacher. Their parents also had nothing in common with the military. Nowadays, almost the entire Earth Federation's male population had to partake in the war — conscription was universal and compulsory, and there were many such young men willing to fight, but just not on the front lines;

that is to say, to become an officer. The army tried to keep its officers safe, at least compared with ordinary soldiers. And besides, in wartime it was possible to make a quick career as an officer, provided you stayed alive. As a result, military academies began to increasingly discriminate in favor of young people from military officer families, seeing this as a kind of a guarantee for those who wanted to be officers by vocation and not for any other reason. In general, the selection process was going to be tough.

In the next few months it was unlikely that I could do much physical activity, so I decided to expand my knowledge of the world to which I had been sent. Igor Lavroff, as expected, knew as much as an average teenager of his civilization and he hitherto hadn't been interested in anything serious and useful for me.

Then, not in the least expecting it, I became interested in xenology, which was Igor's field of study. Since the initial contact with the quargs it was a legitimate science. As a brigadier general I was particularly interested in their army. There was much information on the matter, but I felt it would be difficult to understand without a proper systematization of the data.

The Colonial Technological Institute had an xenology department but after studying the requirements I realized that my current level of knowledge wasn't enough to pass the admission exam. Knowledge about the quargs was available only in this world, so the information put in my brain by Dr Silk couldn't help. I had to make a virtual appointment with Igor's school principal. Of course, I had been absent due to the illness, and they didn't expect my return.

After seeing my application the school principal reached out to me. I don't know what he expected to see, but he was clearly amazed by my appearance.

"Hello, Igor," he said with a slightly strained smile while looking at me. "You're looking fine for a guy with a severe disease."

"No more, Maxim Leonidovich," I returned a smile. "I've not yet recovered, but I'm in rehab after a new treatment."

"That's great news, Igor," the school principal seemed to be really glad. "And when can we expect to see you back at school?"

"That's what I wanted to talk about," I rubbed my nose looking him in the eyes. "Would you kindly look at this," I sent to the school a copy of my biochemistry diploma. I figured there's no need to show the other diplomas.

The principal spent a minute reading the document and then looked at me with an expression of befuddlement and utter incomprehension.

"Igor, but this is… How it's possible?"

"It's a long and complicated story. If you want, I'll tell you sometime. But at the moment I'd like to clarify one point concerning my further studies in school."

"In school?" the principal no longer understood what was going on. "But what for? You already have a higher education, Igor."

"I am interested in xenology, and I want to study it at the Colonial Technological Institute. I need to prepare for the admission exam. I'm now in the hospital and will be here a couple of months. I'd like to study xenology via distance learning."

"Well, I don't know what to say. You've caught me off guard. OK, submit a free-form application to the school. We've got a distance learning course. You won't have to take an exam afterwards. You'll take the institute entry exam instead."

***

Much to my surprise I mastered the xenology course in one day, including the time for writing a placement test to the institute. This made me think hard. Having reached the rank of brigadier general I never considered myself to be a great thinker, and naturally I never was one. Yeah, I had a younger body with a young brain. But this body never before showed itself to be a wonder child.

Apparently, Dr. Silk managed to do something extra with my brain – and with Igor Lavroff's brain - during the direct data download and transfer of senses. Thus, 'our' brain began to work much more intensively. I couldn't help but notice that I could remember the essence of texts when read the very first time, immediately forgetting all the fluff and filler. My reading speed increased five-fold, but my eyes tired from this information flow. Thus, I decided to go easy on using my new capacities in order not to overextend myself and I made sure to take regular breaks while studying.

Nevertheless, six weeks later I passed the final exam at the Colonial Technological Institute and gained access to relevant information on the quargs. As a qualified xenologist I now could work with classified information about the adversary: strategy, tactics, samples of weapons, control systems, electronic warfare, as well as all the vicious shooting equipment and accessories that are so dear to the mind and heart of a commando general and future cadet of the Earth Federation. As part of my postgraduate studies, I now had a right not only to read about the enemy equipment but to touch it and take a look inside. I planned to do that as soon as they let me leave the hospital.

My rehab was coming to an end. Ilya Sergeyevich, who within these two months went from being a provincial doctor to a respectable gentleman thanks to the considerable royalties received, expressed his total satisfaction with the recovery of his dear – in all sense of the word - patient. He was somewhat surprised, however, by my rapid recovery rate. In fact, he said that I could be discharged in a month, but given my case's complexity he wanted to play it safe. I didn't mind since I had much to do.

My personal fly-car was waiting for me in the parking lot near the hospital entrance. I bought it via the net and it came before my discharge. It wasn't a top-of-the-line fly-car, although I could afford to have the best. I don't like to show off even if I have the right to do so. The driving age for such a flying machine here was 14 because the autopilot function prevented accidents.

It took me 20 minutes to fly across the city to get home. Mom prepared dinner. She liked to cook. Home cooking once again became fashionable about 20 years ago. Her food was unusual for me, but it was delicious. I ate it with pleasure while answering mom's questions and sharing my plans with her.

"The Planetary Commando Academy?" mom repeated, struggling with these barbed words. "What for, son? We now have money. We can move into a new house, we can even move to Earth. The professors at the Colonial Technological Institute compete with offers to work with them. You can make an excellent career. Researchers are not drafted into the army. Why this risk? Besides, just look at yourself, what kind of soldier would you make, not to mention a commando?"

"You see, mom, a research career doesn't interest me. Of course, I managed to surprise everyone and to get ahead slightly in this sphere…"

"Slightly? You call slightly — a cure for asteroid fever and four university diplomas at the age of 15?"

"Yes, mom. I call it that. I was able to do it only because I'm terminally ill. I had no other way. But I'm not ready to dedicate my life to it. Research is not for me."

"Well, what is yours? Going off to fight the quargs?" Mom was evidently upset and even raised her voice. "You could be killed there. I've already lost your father although he wasn't a soldier. Losing you is the last thing I need."

"Mom," I replied quietly. "Listen to me, please. I'll do my best not to be killed. I don't want to die, believe me. But I have to do this. The quargs killed my dad. They kill thousands every day. You see what I can do when I put my mind to it. I want to solve the problem of the quargs once and for all, do you see?"

I was amazed with myself while talking. I wasn't telling a tale, not hiding my true goals behind lofty words. All that I told mom was true and I was sincere. Was it a split personality? Or, on the contrary, a confluence of personalities?

Mom watched silently. Then she sobbed quietly but mastered her emotions.

"Where does this come from, son? Your dad was kind and compassionate; not tough and determined. Neither am I. You were different as a child; now you've grown up and you know what? I'm glad. What do you plan to start with?"

"Thanks, mom." I came up, sat near her and put my arm around her shoulders. "You're absolutely right, I see a puny miserable guy when I look in the mirror. I'll fix this first. And I'll study xenology in postgrad. It's important to know one's enemy."

Chapter 4

Those wishing to enter the Planetary Commando Academy had to pass a number of tests, beginning with an interview with military psychologists. I was most concerned with this because of its unpredictability. Based on the interview results the commission made its recommendations: "highly recommended", "recommended", "conditionally recommended" and, lastly, "not recommended". The latter meant it was all over for the candidate. Only about 30 percent of candidates passed this first step, keeping in mind that "conditionally recommended" usually meant "come back next time".

Then they checked if candidates were suitable for military service in accordance with physical and medical fitness standards. Military doctors analyzed medical documents and examined the potential cadets. Physical standards were high, as is the norm for commandos. The commission might say: "unfit for duty" with obvious implications. A score of between 50 and 100 meant you were fit.

After that, they checked a candidate's educational level: tests for math, physics, history and cosmography. I had a hard time with the last two, but my brain's new capacities helped me to solve this in one week. I managed to reach a higher level of knowledge than was necessary to enter the Academy.

The Planetary Commando Academy was located on Ganymede. I arrived there a day before exams began. I had sent all the necessary paperwork to the admissions office. Ganymede had been colonized by Europeans. I didn't notice any difference compared to Titan, except that Saturn and not Jupiter occupied half the sky at night. It was also clearly visible during the day. Some people considered Saturn to be the Solar System's most beautiful planet, but I liked Jupiter more.

As for the artificial thermonuclear sun, it was just like the one near Titan - revolving round Ganymede and imitating the 24 hour day-night cycle and seasonal changes. A gravity adjustor embedded in the rocky thickness of the moon maintained Earth's normal gravity for the comfort of the inhabitants. English was, predictably, the main language here. Thanks to Igor Lavroff, I knew it well.

I settled in the Academy dorm. I could have gotten a hotel room, but I wanted to revisit my youth when after the orphanage and Imperial military school I entered Commando Military College where one graduated as a junior non-commissioned officer. At that time I lived in a dorm room shared with two raucous guys just like me. As it turned out, the rooms were for one person only, but that didn't bother me. I felt a bit tired after my journey and I abandoned my plan to read something before the interview. So, I hit the sack.

Next morning, a group of candidates gathered in the hall, and then in a formation we were taken to a waiting area where there were around 40 people. Not all the candidates were present; those wishing to undergo tests were divided into several groups to avoid pandemonium. I was surprised by the procedure's archaic nature.

The auditorium door opened from time to time, and the commission secretary stepped out to call a candidate's name and said to come in. This was a long-standing tradition. Igor Lavroff's memory hadn't retained such details and it didn't occur to me to inquire. The interview results weren't immediately announced. A candidate exited the auditorium, took a seat and waited until everyone was interviewed.

I was called near the end. The secretary walked me to the table where three officers in their fifties sat: a colonel and two Lt. colonels. Their bars impressed me, indicating their combat experience and level of theoretical knowledge. I figured that professors at a military academy in a warring state should be just like that.

I stood at attention.

"Candidate Lavroff reporting for the entrance exam."

"Sit down, candidate."

I sat and was ready to answer, but first I had to listen to the Colonel's speech.

"So, this is candidate Lavroff. It should be noted he's an unusual candidate - with four university diplomas, not to mention currently doing postgrad in xenology at the Colonial Technological Institute on Titan. Please pay attention, sirs," he said, addressing the lieutenant colonels. "This candidate is entitled to an exemption from conscription, but still, he came to us. That's not all. As far as we know, and we know it for certain, none of your ancestors have ever been a military professional. What do you want here, candidate Lavroff?"

I was prepared for this question and long ago had chosen persuasive arguments. Oddly enough, it was based upon my conversation with mom one year prior.

"I have a score to settle with the quargs, Sir. My father died in the Van Maanen star system six years ago. An enemy destroyer torpedoed his transport ship."

"We know and extend our sympathy," the colonel answered in an unemotional voice. "But we consider this reason to be totally insufficient for a candidate to enter our Academy. A thirst for revenge, however righteous it may be, is not what we do here. You could be much more useful doing scientific research instead of being a commando. You can make new weapons and technologies — that way you could kill more of the enemy instead of shooting them yourself or heading a commando unit. Do you have anything specific to object to, candidate?"

"Yes, Sir. I fully agree; it's possible to kill as you mentioned, but some scores must be settled looking the enemy in the eye. That's my approach."

"Is that all?"

"May I continue, Sir?" I waited for a nod from the Colonel. "I got my first three diplomas for one reason - I was ill with asteroid fever, which until recently was incurable. I had no other option except to find a cure myself. I felt that I could do it, and here I am. I'm healthy."

The Colonel turned to one of his subordinates.

"Is that so?"

"That's right, Sir. Candidate Lavroff is one of the holders of the patent on asteroid fever treatment and his surname is first on the patent application.

"Go on, candidate."

"I have a goal, Sir, and it's not a research career. I want to finish the war with the quargs in my lifetime, and to fight for complete victory. I want our troops to land on their mother planet and conquer it. My goal is to lead this operation."

"Modesty isn't a problem for you," wryly remarked one of the lieutenant colonels.

"Those aren't empty words, Lt. Colonel, Sir," I replied calmly. "I can set goals and achieve them. Look at me. The fact that I'm alive is proof of this statement. And I've told you my goal."

The Colonel stared right at me.

"A Russian commander once remarked: a bad soldier is one who doesn't dream of becoming a general. Do you mean that's your case?"

"It's not like that, Sir. I'd phrase it differently. A bad soldier is one who doesn't know WHY he wants to become a general. I know why."

"Do you have any other questions for candidate Lavroff, Sirs?"

"It seems we've heard enough, Colonel, Sir."

"In this case you're free to go, candidate."

I left the auditorium, and the door closed behind the next candidate who went in to be interviewed. All right, I did everything I could, now I have to wait until the interviews finish and to know the outcome.

The last cadet applicant left the auditorium 40 minutes later. Nothing happened for half an hour; then we were all lined up to hear the results.

The Colonel came forward with his tablet and started to read out surnames and the commission's recommendations. The net forums didn't lie. The great majority of candidates received the commission's opinion: "not recommended". Some five guys got "conditionally recommended" and were glad. Three guys and one girl, who at the moment looked as if they were already commandos, received "recommended". Only two remained: myself and a flaxen-haired lad a bit taller than myself, and who was one of the first to enter the auditorium.

"Candidate Petrenko," the Colonel pronounced the flaxen-haired lad's last name. "The commission postpones a decision on your candidacy due to a request for additional documents about your relationship with the police of Callisto from the archives. The decision will be announced tomorrow at the same time."

The guy looked despondent. Apparently, the mentioned relationship had indeed taken place and couldn't possibly help his biography.

"Candidate Lavroff," the Colonel looked Igor in the eye. "The commission has considered your case with great care and concluded that your qualities can be of use to the planetary commandos. The verdict is: 'highly recommended'."

While I was leaving the Academy somebody called my last name. I turned around and saw three guys and the girl who had got a "recommended". I stopped and waited for them to catch up.

"I'm Inga," the girl introduced herself. "And these are my friends: Mike, Stephen and Chen. We studied together on Earth, at Canberra."

"Igor," I presented myself and remembered that there was an infantry school in Australia. "So, you're already sergeants."

"Yes, we are," responded bluntly a big guy with a broad round face that wasn't at all a clever-looking one. "We're staff sergeants. We studied for two years at the Australian Mobile Infantry School and were top graduates. Our parents are officers and we have outstanding recommendations for the Academy. And who are you? You're a civilian…"

"Stephen!" Inga interjected. "Keep your cool. We just wanted to ask…"

"No! Let him answer. There'll be new tests tomorrow. And some of our guys who earned the right to study here won't pass because of this civilian upstart," Stephen made a threatening step toward me, but Chen laid an arm on his shoulder and Mike held him by the elbow.

"Stephen, calm down," Mike said, sounding a bit tense. "If you fight now at the Academy entrance then all of us will get kicked out of here before tomorrow's tests. Wait a little. If candidate Lavroff fails the tests then there'll be nothing to worry about. If not, you'll still have many chances to ask him various questions."

Stephen removed the arm off his shoulder and regained control of himself, although he continued to stare at me with animosity.

"Igor, excuse us, please," Inga said, looking annoyed with her friends. "We just want to know why the commission liked you so much? You don't strike us as a candidate for an officer-commando."

"I simply explained to them," I responded, shrugging my shoulders, "my goals and objectives as a future Federation officer. I just found the right words. Excuse me, lady and gentlemen, but I got to go."

I nodded, turned and moved toward the fly-car's parking spot, while feeling unfriendly eyes looking at my back.

Next morning I again stood before a commission. This time it was a medical one. A tall and rather young medical lieutenant colonel carefully studied my medical chart on his tablet without offering me to sit down. Finally, he looked up at me.

"Asteroid fever? How does it feel to be a living corpse, candidate?"

"It's a really nasty feeling, Lt. Colonel, Sir, but it focuses and motivates you," I gave him a half-smile.

"I've heard of you. But I've got some bad news, candidate. While the commission has no issues with the state of your health, since you suffered not long ago from a serious illness, which until recently was considered incurable, you're starting with minus 30 points according to the rules. Do you wish to continue?"

That was a low blow. Even if I had perfect scores in all the exercises, which was very unlikely, I'd only get 70 points at the most. Still, I wasn't going to back down.

"That's right, Lt. Colonel, Sir," I tried to keep my voice calm. "Do I have your permission to continue the testing ?"

"Hmm…, you can take a hit, candidate. Well, let's look at what you can do. Sergeant, he's yours."

The first test was a five-kilometer cross-country race. I didn't have a problem with that - I was good at running and I easily beat the time. Difficulties then ensued, however. I had a couple of minutes to catch my breath after running and the sergeant sent me to the pull-up bar.

I did 20, but right after I had to do push-ups and only managed 53; when rested, I could do 80 push-ups.

Weightlifting and throwing heavy objects – those were the worst for me - and now it was my turn. Weights were never my forte. I could barely lift the minimum. My muscles, the lucky owner of which I happened to be, were perfect for body weight exercises, as well as for long distance running, swimming, martial arts and many other things useful for a commando, but not for heavy loads.

Maybe the doctor was right and I hadn't fully recovered from the disease, but I preferred not to think about that. The next test was grenade throwing. I had to throw mock grenades, trying to hit rectangular targets the size of an adult's torso that appeared out of the ground at varying distances.

I had to hit as many as possible in a minute. Then my body surprised me again. I never knew I had a talent for this, and I hit the bulls-eye each time. Except there was one problem: I couldn't throw a grenade to the farthest targets. I was lucky to have just 10 percent of targets like that, but I lost time waiting for new targets to appear instead of those I couldn't reach. Overall, the results weren't disappointing, and the sergeant looked approvingly at the "enemies" that I had destroyed.

After that came a flexibility test, a balance test, a vestibular function test, and a motor coordination test. I passed all of them. The final test was martial arts. I was told that no one would kill or maim me, but I shouldn't expect any favors. The trainer's attacks would gradually increase, and the goal was to hold out as long as possible, staying within the ring and not getting knocked out of it. A candidate had the right to tap out if, for example, the trainer applied an armlock.

The tests were taken individually so I didn't see how other candidates performed. The Sergeant led me to the middle of a hexagonal area and left me. It was a typical lawn delineated by white lines. Along one of the sides was a comfortable bench, vacant at the moment. That was all.

I decided to use the downtime to stretch and warm-up my feet and knees. A few minutes later I saw the examiners. There were four: a major in uniform who I hadn't met before, and three officers – the members of the very first commission with whom I had an interview. I continued to warm up while they slowly approached, and when they were close I stood at attention.

"You're warming up, candidate?" said the Colonel after hearing my report. "Here's your trainer, Major Steinitz. Are you aware of the exam terms?"

"Yes, Colonel, Sir," I responded without delay.

"Remember, fatal and mutilating blows can only be imitated; full contact blows are prohibited. A clean hit to a specified target zone means victory. Aside from that, do whatever you need to do in order to remain as long as possible in the marked area. Is that understood, candidate?"

"That's right, Colonel, Sir," I repeated.

"Then, let's get started. Major, you're in charge."

Steinitz took a long look at me. I returned the favor. The Major slightly raised one eyebrow, although maybe I just imagined it.

"That will be your starting point," the trainer said, indicating the opposite side of the area with his hand. "We begin at my order."

The distance between us was about eight meters. I closely watched my opponent trying to imagine what fighting style he'd follow. Steinitz was five centimeters taller and about 15 kilos heavier. He was undoubtedly well-trained and moved smoothly, but I felt his slow movements were misleading and could at any moment result in a series of quick strikes and kicks or jumps.

For 10 months before trying to enter the Academy I did my best to whip my body into shape. In my previous life I practiced several forms of martial arts. It turned out that my new body partially retained those skills, but its potential didn't match its skills, lacking flexibility and muscle strength, let alone endurance.

Igor Lavroff's feeble body couldn't even imagine the brutality of the master who now possessed it. This body had really taken a beating. As soon as the rehab period was over I immediately joined a gym where I trained and exercised so hard that I crawled home on all fours. Mom just shook her head sadly, but six months later I started to notice that she was pleased with me.

Dr. Silk had given me information about this activity. In theory, I knew more than 10 martial arts, of which I only heard about before. But to utilize acquired knowledge wasn't as easy as practicing what I knew previously. That's why I decided to concentrate on those things that were most effective or unexpected for a potential adversary. Now was the time to try out that full array of skills.

"Action," said the Major, and out of the corner of my eye I saw that the Colonel started a stopwatch.

The trainer didn't play for time because his goal was to quickly take out a candidate. But this was an exam and if the trainer knocked out a candidate on the first strike, he wouldn't be able to ascertain his level. That's why he started with a two-handed attack to my head. I defended myself stepping back and did not counterattack. There was no point in disclosing my full potential right away. It'd be imprudent to expect to defeat this well-trained adversary, and if I showed him my real level of training he'd certainly quickly go at me harder. Time – that meant everything to me at the moment. Time meant points that I had to battle for.

The second attack was quicker, although he evidently was holding back. For the moment the trainer acted directly: he made no feints, but attacked me from various distances. This time Steinitz started with a kick to the upper part of my leg and then a quick transition to a hand attack to my head and torso. I managed to get my leg from under the kick, but found myself near the border line, so I had to quickly move aside to defend myself from his punches. I didn't counterattack again. It wasn't time for that. In general, it seemed prudent to mirror the trainer's skills and to demonstrate my own capabilities in fending off the current threat.

As it turned out I wasn't this trainer's first wiseass, and the next attack was twice as fast as the previous, preceded by a feint imitating a punch in my head. So, I had to fight back in earnest. I slightly strayed to the right from the feint, then handled the forthcoming ankle trip, putting my support foot up just in time to let go of my adversary's undercutting leg and block a very quick punch to the liver.

After he closed the distance, I went on the offensive to stop him continuing an attack that might have dire consequences. I countered with an elbow strike to the shoulder joint that's quite effective against heavier adversaries. My goal was to push the Major aside, not so much to hit him. This move apparently was unexpected and when the trainer noticed my blow he cushioned it by moving slightly aside. He had to break his attack, which was exactly what I hoped for.

Once again a space opened between us. The Major made short feigning motions and tried to push me to the edge. Seeing how I remained passive, he tried to force an attack in order to intercept me. I realized I couldn't back down forever. I felt we had been fighting for about a minute. A stopwatch beep from the Colonel's tablet confirmed I was right. I had met the minimum requirement. Still, I couldn't but remember the penalty of 30 points due to asteroid fever, which seemed to be getting its revenge even after my recovery.

When the first minute of combat was over, the trainer felt he had free rein. He continued to goad me to attack, not allowing me to get into the open. Well, I can also feint. I made a short quick step forward and raised my front leg slightly imitating a kick to his torso. An experienced fighter, the trainer understood that I wasn't going to kick. He didn't dodge my feint but made a step ahead in order to intercept me. Then the Major crouched and quickly jabbed me in the solar plexus while holding his right hand ready against a possible left foot kick. He was a true professional, and I wasn't able to parry his jab but managed to move aside a bit.

Steinitz's fist skittered along my ribs without hitting anything vital. Still, my side exploded with pain. My situation was dire because I couldn't move back as I was close to the line. My awkward stance after trying to dodge his blow meant that I couldn't move left. I was anxious to move right since I didn't want to run into an oncoming kick or punch that he could pull off in his current stance. I could only do a short distance counter-attack. Against a much heavier adversary this almost always ends in defeat. Since this was not a sporting event, however, one could do anything he wanted, though making sure to control the force of the blow.

So, I quickly poked my fingers into the pressure points on the neck, clavicle and axillary crease of my adversary. The major instantaneously assessed the threat and moved fast to keep me from hitting the target. But his stance became less stable, which was the goal of my desperate attack. I finished by pushing him in the chest with an open palm instead of poking my fingers for the fourth time.

If I tried it immediately then I wouldn't be able to dislodge my heavy adversary from his position. The Major hadn't lost his balance, but he had to take a step back, opening the way to my freedom. I jumped to the right and made a roll-over, and found myself in the middle. I got a kick in the back, but his leg moved in pursuit of me, hence the kick wasn't that strong. I wasn't even out of breath. I leapt up and turned around to face my adversary. Major Steinitz smiled, nodded and turned to the commission.

"Colonel, Sir, candidate Lavroff passed the test. We're not going to kill him, and if I don't kill him, he'll just keep running from me."

"Hmm, I was not expecting that," said the Colonel making a note on his tablet. "But you understand this issue better, Major."

Looking up at me, he added: "You're free to go. We'll tell you the result later."

Chapter 5

As it turned out the fight with major Steinitz saved me from a swift departure. I got the highest grade and my total for medical tests and physical training was 53. That wasn't just low, it was very low. My chances to be a cadet were fading fast.

General aptitude tests were held over the next four days. The difficulty level of the mathematics and physics exams made me smile. The examiners didn't bother with additional questions because they feared I knew the subject better than they did. Apparently, they had read my file. Their concerns were justified, but I was quite proper with them and didn't show off the level of my knowledge. No need to embarrass people and make enemies. It looked like my behavior was appreciated, and I got the highest score in both exams.

There were no problems with cosmography and history, although I wasn't able to outwit the professors. Nevertheless, they were satisfied with my knowledge.

The admission committee's final decision was to be announced the day after the last theoretical exam. Based on the results each candidate got an integral score that summarized the grades he received in all tests, as well as bonus points for extra knowledge and skills. The passing grade was calculated on the basis of the number of places available in the Academy. This time it was equal to 282. That was a lot and there were eight candidates for each spot. And no one ever got conclusions such as "unfit" or "not recommended".

I received 100 points for the entrance exam and 100 for the general aptitude exams; my score was 53 for the medical tests and physical training. Also, I was given extra points for my university diplomas, but only for physics and medicine. Xenology and biochemistry were not valued at the Academy. All in all, I got 273 points, nine less than needed.

I was going to return to my dorm and pack, but the candidates weren't yet relieved from the hall where they gathered to hear the results announced. As it turned out, I was hasty with my conclusions. I hadn't noticed something earlier: a candidate who had received an "highly recommended" on the entrance exam could count on an individual decision provided he fell short by no more than 15 points. There were five of us in this group: four guys and one gal.

A somber sergeant showed us to the Academy director's office. Lt. General Shiller, a big graying man with a heavy chin, listened to the sergeant's report and gave him a nod. Then he looked at us.

"So, candidates. Admit it: you blew it," he said with mild neglect, looking at his tablet. "You're five, and only one will be a cadet; the rest go home. Candidate Yakovleva, let's start with you. You failed physical training. You've got no strength, no reaction, no combat skills. But you have flexibility, a good vestibular system, coordination and endurance. Your total is 268. You've got three minutes to convince me why you should be a planetary commando. You can mention any of your skills and abilities that weren't considered when calculating your score. If they're relevant, I might add some points to your score. Any questions?"

"No questions, Lt. General, Sir."

"All right, Go."

I liked the girl. She looked self-assured and had a pleasant and unordinary appearance, although she was not particularly beautiful.

"I'm a speleologist, not a professional, but a high-level certified specialist. I don't suffer from claustrophobia. I can orient in complete darkness anywhere, including dilapidated bunkers and other underground structures. In caves as well, of course. I got experience in diving, including flooded tunnels."

"Is that all, candidate?"

"Yes."

"I have to disappoint you - you're not a match for the academy. These skills aren't vital for a commando. I can add five points for your ability to orient in dilapidated bunkers – after checking. But it won't change anything. That's all, candidate Yakovleva," the general looked at his tablet again. "Now, candidate Wu Chi Zung. You practically failed physics and maths. Your total score is 270."

A short Vietnamese man stepped forward.

"You've got three minutes, candidate. You're on the clock."

"Lt. General, Sir," he spoke English almost with no accent, "I'm a tracker. A very good one. I can find my way in the jungle, cross swamps and water barriers, I've got experience surviving in a tropical forest without equipment and food. I can make missiles out of available materials. I'm a good archer, can shoot a crossbow, as well as throw knives and hatchets. The rest was considered in the evaluation."

The General reflected on this.

"I can't say that our army doesn't need you. I'm even ready to write you a recommendation to another Academy. Commando and saboteur are different specializations. A commando might be in a situation when your skills are needed. But that's not often. Still, I'll give you a chance. I'll add 12 points to equal your result with the passing score. If none of the three remaining candidates gets more, you'll be a cadet. Afterwards, your skills will be checked. Go back."

The general looked at the three candidates left and checked his notes.

"Candidate Lavroff."

I stepped forward.

"So, you failed …" the General looked at his tablet and was puzzled. "Well, it turns out that you didn't fail anything. You got minus 30 points for the medical. Why are you here with a score like this? Your total is 273. Ok. Go ahead."

"Lt. General, Sir, besides the diplomas included in the evaluation I have two more higher education degrees: in biochemistry and xenology."

"I'll add five points for xenology. It could be of use to an officer, but it's not critical. Anything else?"

"I know the quargs' ground military equipment, small arms, light weapons and guided missiles. I can make minor repairs and maintenance as well as program control systems. I can operate some of their machines." The latter claim was a bit exaggerated, but modesty wasn't necessary now.

"Well," the General considered this for a moment and started to look for something on his tablet. "What is this?"

On the screen I saw a machine that's called a walking tank in my world. However, this name never stuck here.

"This is a light infantry support assault robot known as the 'Small Dragon'. It's a single-seater, with a 32mm automatic gun, an automatic grenade launcher, two surface-to-air missiles in the backpack launcher and a short-range flame thrower on the right shoulder joint. The fire control system includes front and upper hemisphere scanners and a controller for automatic tracking and target classification. The fire control system ensures simultaneous engagement of different targets using various weapons by priority."

"That's enough," said the General, clicking on the virtual keyboard icon. "Major Ignatoff, report to my office."

Five minutes later I took the elevator all the way to the Academy's lowest basement level. The elevator doors opened. The Major and I exited and saw a spacious hangar poorly illuminated by ceiling lamps.

"Here it is, our trophy," said the Major, showing me a combat robot in the corner. "The Small Dragon. The Lt. General said you're familiar with it."

"That's right, Major, I'm familiar with it."

"Our commandos captured it during an assault on a quarg base in the Beta Canum Venaticorum system. It was still in factory packaging. We took many trophies there. Lt. General Shilller got his hands on this one and has been using it as a demo unit for our cadets. We got into the cabin, but couldn't do much else. The controls are locked, and to call in a technician from Earth – it's too far and expensive. You want to get into the cabin?"

"Yes, I need to check something."

"Go ahead."

I got into the cabin using the clamps on the robot's left leg and looked around. Everything was familiar. I had spent much time rummaging in the insides of quarg combat machines, but they always were damaged. This one was brand new. It had all the connectors and ports, so I didn't test the major's patience and climbed out.

"Major, Sir, I've got some useful equipment, but it's in my dorm room. If you give me permission to go get it then I'll tame this Dragon in just three hours with help from two competent technicians and a mobile repair kit."

"Really? Then wait a bit."

The Major stepped aside, talked to someone on his communicator and returned.

"Candidate, you have 30 minutes. Be here at 14:10. Repair technicians will be waiting for you. The commander is interested, don't disappoint him."

"Your permission to carry it out?"

"Do it."

Two technicians, both warrant officers in their late thirties, at first treated me suspiciously. But after spending 40 minutes to take the enemy robot half apart with my help and under my instructions, their doubts dissipated and they were enthusiastic. These guys loved their work, and it was very interesting for them to participate in dissecting an alien machine.

As soon as we reached the circuits that I needed I took out the equipment made on Titan during my postgrad studies, and started to cautiously connect adapters to the Dragon's technical slots. I connected the robot's electronics with a set of computers that converted the programming code I had written into a sequence of commands that was normally understood by quarg machines.

My program utilized a security vulnerability that existed in an access system via technical ports. It was impossible to control a robot while in the cabin without the appropriate digital keys. To repair a damaged robot the quargs used technical ports inside it where the defense system was considerably weaker. It wasn't designed to repel the sophisticated hacking methods from my world that was 200 years ahead of this one.

Anyway, when the elevator doors opened three hours later, and Major Ignatoff and Lieutenant General Shiller came into the hangar, our small team was polishing the Small Dragon for the tenth time after carefully cleaning it of industrial residues that we used during disassembly and assembly.

When the brass appeared we jumped down from the robot, forming a short line, by age and length of service. The warrant officer reported: "Lt. General, Sir, the technical team has finished reconditioning the Small Dragon combat robot within the established time frame."

"Candidate Lavroff!"

"That's me," I said energetically while taking a step forward.

"Show us the result of your efforts."

"Yes, Sir," I responded and turned to the robot.

I wouldn't say that I felt comfortable sitting in the cabin. The quargs are smaller than humans, and their anatomy differs from ours. They have seven long flexible fingers, their arms are about 10 centimeters shorter than ours. Their legs are, on the contrary, longer. Their head is similar to ours in terms of basic features: they have the same two ears, a mouth, nose and eyes. But they're not attractive at all. Who likes the bluish skin of a horror film zombie that's full of wrinkles, and which was on a diet and had lost half of its weight in two days. But they were good fighters and very dangerous enemies.

I sat down in an uncomfortable chair, and connected my tablet to the system. I put a frame down that served as safety restraints on my shoulders. My arms and legs felt the clamps of the exoskeleton's control system that allowed the robot to repeat all my body movements. The exoskeleton smoothly assumed the position of the Dragon's current stance. My tablet made a sound that everything was ready. The systems test went well and the robot was ready for action.

I turned to the officers, took two steps towards them, turning the body to the right, then to the left. I slightly raised the robotic right arm and aimed the gun at the hangar's far side. By the way, there was sufficient ammo. These machines were apparently shipped to fighting units with the ammo already loaded. That carried a certain risk, and we wouldn't do that. But who really knows the quargs? They probably tried to decrease the time to prepare the machine for combat, but that didn't do much good with this particular specimen.

I continued to walk about, making combative poses and demonstrating the robot's capabilities. I intended to bring it back to its place, but the general signaled to stop. He told the technicians to do something and they ran to the far side of the hangar, returning with four crash helmets. Obeying a remote command the hangar's far wall moved slowly aside and I saw a wide corridor that was approximately 200 meters long. Three targets resembling the quargs' fighting space-suits appeared at the end of the corridor. Officers and technicians put the crash helmets on, and the general pointed to the targets.

I never before fired enemy weapons, but these were really good conditions to try. The general was interested in seeing if I could control all the machine's systems. Well, I was really happy to have this chance, and I brought the machine to the firing line. The quargs' targeting interface bothered me. Their eyesight was surprisingly similar to ours, but their perception... Actually, I spent a lot of time during my postgraduate studies trying to adapt myself to it.

Intersecting circles and polygons of different colors chaotically floated before my eyes. It could be anything, just not a targeting system, and that's why practice is important. I slightly raised the robotic right arm and destroyed the two outermost targets with single shots. The shells shattered them into fragments. To destroy the third I used a grenade, estimating in advance that the explosion wasn't dangerous for the spectators. I was happy with the result. The central target was obliterated. A blast wave, weakened by the distance, came from the corridor, slightly shaking the Dragon.

After returning the machine to its departure position, I slipped out of the cabin and ran to the officers.

"Lt. General, Sir..."

"At ease, Cadet Lavroff. Thank you for your service."

"Serving the Earth Federation," I answered cheerfully with great relief.

"Finish your affairs in the civilian world, cadet. You have two days. You'll be sent a copy of the admission order and other details. You're free to go."

I returned to my dorm room in high spirits. Luck was on my side. I was slightly dejected only by the fact that without luck, as well as a string of fortunate coincidences, I might have failed. This must be taken into consideration for the future. I can't fail; so, I can't depend on luck. Still, I knew deep down that this was just a pious wish, no more than that. Chance can play an important role in one's life. Sometimes you can't wait for luck, but must risk in order to win. Or you lose while risking nothing and then regret it for the rest of your life.

A low voice interrupted my thoughts: "Cadet Lavroff, could I have two minutes?"

I turned back. In the shadow of a decorative plant stood Chen, one of those guys who had stopped his friend from a reckless brawl at the Academy entrance. He leaned against the corridor wall feeling relaxed.

"Sure, Chen, to what do I owe the honor?"

"Cadet, you were wrong to have had an argument with Stephen."

"I didn't quarrel with him. I didn't even have a chance to tell him anything."

"Stephen's best friend, Mike, who was with us that time, didn't pass the exam. He flies back to Earth, but Stephen, Inga and I are cadets, just like you. Stephen is furious and thinks Mike didn't make the Academy because of guys like you."

"And you, Chen, do you also think that?"

"Of course, not," he smiled slightly. "But Stephen is my friend since school in Australia, and I don't want him to be thrown out of the Academy because of a fight with you. Just be more careful with him. He's hot-tempered and intense. He's only on good behavior with superiors and old friends like Mike and Inga. Plus, his father is an admiral at the General Staff, and from time to time he checks up on his son, and will get involved when the need arises."

"Thanks for the info, but why tell me all this?"

Chen grinned.

"You can't even imagine what Stephen can do when he's upset. If he hates someone he'll do everything to make that man's life hell. But he usually just ends up creating hell for both himself and that of his closest friends. I've been through this before and I don't want to go through it again. Anyway, don't piss him off. But that's entirely up to you."

"Chen, it's not my business, but why are you with him?"

"Let's say there's a certain debt that's not easy to pay back, and that keeps me here. So, I'm not going anywhere. At least not yet. And if it comes to a direct confrontation don't count on my help or even my sympathy."

"Hmmm, at least you're honest," I grinned. "I won't promise anything, but I heard what you said."

"That's all I expected. Good luck, Cadet," Chen smiled once again and headed slowly towards the exit.

***

How does a military academy freshman's morning begin? Correct! With the alarm clock, washing-up and a morning run followed by more exercise. I even had a slight feeling of déjà vu, but there were some differences in the pattern that I remembered from my previous life.

When my group stood near a lecture hall waiting for math class, a sergeant instructor called me and took me aside.

"Cadet Lavroff," he said. "By order of the Academy director you are exempt from attending math and physics classes. Instead, you'll have special lessons with Major Ignatoff and Major Steinitz. Now, I'll escort you to the place of your first individual lesson."

We took the elevator down to the hangar that I was already familiar with. Major Ignatoff was waiting near the quarg combat robot. The Sergeant went about his business, and the Major said smiling: "Cadet Lavroff, congratulations on acceptance into our Academy. I wasn't able to do so in person before," he held out his hand to shake mine. I was surprised. Actually, I was going to stand at attention and shout according to army regulations, 'Serving the Earth Federation!'"

"Thank you, Major, Sir," I shook his hand.

"You'll see, cadet. This won't be a usual class. I won't teach you anything, at least not now. You'll teach me. What do we have here now? We have a combat machine in our Academy and one man who can control it, and that man is neither an instructor nor a professor; he's not even a technician, he's a freshman. I believe you'll agree this isn't normal. Let's correct this state of affairs. Are you ready?"

"Yes, Sir."

"Leave it, Cadet. It's just the two of us here now, and I allow you to speak to me without formalities. This will simplify the training. Let's begin, Cadet."

"I'm ready, but I'll need access to your tablet in order to install the necessary software. And I'll need special equipment that's in my dorm room."

The Major turned out to be a good student and he was a fast learner. I didn't bother to teach him how to hack the robot's protection system, but instead concentrated on how to use the machine, guidance and navigation devices, weapons and other equipment needed by a pilot in a combat machine. Ignatoff took his time and didn't hesitate to ask when he didn't understand something.

Simulators were often used to imitate a combat machine on the battlefield in order to train pilots for the Earth Federation's robots. But there were no such simulators for a captured combat machine. So the Major had to train in a real combat machine, and I had to guide his actions via the communicator from outside since the Small Dragon had a one-man cab.

Nevertheless, during our second lesson Major Ignatoff cautiously conducted the Small Dragon along the hangar's perimeter. By the end of the fourth lesson he was moving pretty good in any direction, including reversing and lateral driving. A week later he was able to jump and to change direction quickly. On the whole, the Major had a pretty good handle on the robot.

During our second week we mastered the robot's weapons, and Ignatoff secured permission for us to use the Academy's firing range, which was located 400 kilometers from the city. We had to fly there on a dropship, and it was lots of fun. This practice was very helpful and there was no shortage of ammo.

As it turned out the commandos managed to obtain a lot of ammo at the same quarg warehouse from which the Small Dragon was captured. We shot targets with the gun and grenade launcher: both stationary and in motion, aiming at fixed and moving targets. Lt. General Shiller generously provided us with four simulators for Heron enemy attack planes. The Major and I gladly destroyed the air targets one after another using missiles from the backpack launcher.

As a result, by the end of the second week after returning from the firing range, I looked at Major Ignatoff who resembled a satisfied tomcat with a jug of cream that he just devoured, and said: "Major, it seems there's nothing more I can teach you. You handle the Small Dragon just as well as I do."

"That's debatable," answered the Major, who was apparently happy with my assessment of his skills. "You're right, Cadet. From now on I can improve on my own. Major Steinitz approached me twice asking when I could hand you over to him in order to be torn to pieces. So tomorrow you'll go to him."

"Certainly."

"Here's what I'll add, Cadet. First, thanks for the training. You certainly have the skills of an instructor. Second, if you need my assistance address me unofficially in person without the chain of command. I just sent you my contact info."

My tablet vibrated, indicating an incoming message.

"Thank you, Major, Sir. Your permission to ask a question?"

"Go ahead, Cadet."

"Why can't the Academy train cadets to use captured weapons and equipment? Commandos often lose contact with the main force and can't be supplied with ammo and needed repairs; or reinforcements can't arrive in time. Captured weapons and equipment is the only chance to do the job, or just stay alive."

"What do you think, cadet?"

"The problem is that our commandos don't know how to make the enemy equipment obey new masters."

"That's correct, Cadet. It's impossible to do this in the field."

"But we've just returned from the firing range where we made the Small Dragon do everything we wanted, and it obeyed us. It took three hours to hack it, which is acceptable in an airborne landing operation."

"Where are we supposed to get a certified xenologue specializing in quarg combat machines? You'll need someone in each battalion, otherwise there's no point."

"You don't need a xenologue, Major. I can train the two technicians I worked with; in a week they'll be able to hack another Dragon. No need to develop hacking software and do special research as I did. They'll get ready-to-use, regularly updated programs and instructions. They just need a set of special equipment and adapters to connect our human devices to interface of the quargs' machines. Any battalion technician can do this. No need for a separate unit, but commandos will have to be taught how to handle the hacked machines and equipment."

The Major looked at me with interest but didn't respond at once.

"Sounds encouraging," he said. "But it requires serious consideration. Anyway, I can't make these decisions. Let's do it this way: put this all in writing, I'll read it, think it over and decide how best to present it to the Academy director. I'll write a report and we'll see. I need it tonight. Can you do that?"

"Certainly."

"Then you're free to go, Cadet."

Chapter 6

Naturally, I was not exempt from attending other classes, and during these two weeks I was busy studying military science with the others in my platoon. I got lucky again: Stephen was assigned to another platoon. However, Inga, another participant of that memorable incident at the Academy's entrance, was appointed our platoon commander since she was a senior sergeant.

A squad was the basic tactical unit in Earth Federation's troops. A commando squad consisted of 10 soldiers and a light combat robot, Goanna-M2. Three of these 10 commandos had heavy armored space suits and the necessary weapons. All the rest fought in light armor and with firearms. When landing on an enemy-occupied planet a dropship brought the squad to the surface. It also served as a transport ship there and if necessary provided cover with its guns. A dropship couldn't return to orbit on its own and a special landing transport ship was needed to evacuate it from the surface. We learned all this in tactical class and we trained hard to get in and out of a dropship at the firing range, but one which never flew. I seriously doubted that this dropship could get into the air. It probably did some time ago, but not now.

Each cadet had to be able to perform any task needed in a squad, including piloting the dropship and operating a combat robot. After graduating the Academy a cadet certainly will become an officer and command at least a platoon, but the Academy expected that an officer be able to do everything a soldier can do, which I think is right.

Inga was indifferent towards me and Stephen's outburst apparently had no effect on her, which was good. When we trained in our squads I didn't see her much. Then, when my classes with Major Ignatoff ended I was unexpectedly promoted to squad commander, which became a headache and which meant that I saw Inga more often.

***

Major Steinitz received me differently than Ignatoff. Having heard my report, he said: "Let's go, cadet, I'll show you something."

We entered a large room in the center of which was a holographic projector. Steinitz turned it on and a stereoscopic picture of the sparring area appeared, the same place where the Major and I faced off. I was able to see our fight as a spectator. Of course, the difference in our abilities was clear, but I wasn't surprised at all. I was wondering why the Major was showing me our fight. Suddenly, the playback speed slowed drastically and the image stopped completely.

"Pay attention to this moment, Cadet. Here I could have killed you."

I saw it. In the still Steinitz jabbed me in the torso. I tried to dodge it and I succeeded, although only partially, because Steinitz deliberately didn't alter the trajectory of his blow. The speed of my sideway movement allowed him to hit me in the chest, and not just skitter along my ribs, as it was during the fight. In that case his blow would have been strong enough to seriously damage my heart.

"What do you see?"

I answered him.

"You know much, and can do too much for your age and level of physical training," said the Major after pausing a second. "I read your file carefully and then I made further enquiries through my network. In the past year you studied with three masters: Li Chang, Ilya Proskuroff and Bill Baker. I won't even try to guess how much it cost you, but you're not poor as far as I know."

"That's right, Major, Sir. The royalties allow my family not to worry about money."

"I know. So, I spoke to two of your teachers, and both, independently of each other, told me that they suspect you had already seriously studied martial arts before, but none could identify what kind of fighting style you had. Look here," and Steinitz showed me a fragment of the video of our fight where I countered him with an elbow strike to the shoulder joint and thus was able to create some space and escape from a dangerous attack. "I didn't know this tactical technique; that's why you managed to escape. So, I agree with your trainers."

The Major turned off the projector and turned to me.

"By whom and when were you taught to fight?"

"I was born and raised on Titan, Major, Sir. My whole life is an open book. There are no hidden parts in it. You are well aware that I never studied martial arts before becoming ill. I only did sports as part of the mandatory school curriculum."

"I see you're not lying here, as your physical condition makes it clear that you haven't had serious training for years. In addition to muscles, there are motor skills. You do a lot of moves automatically and that can't be achieved in just 10 months of training. Besides, you didn't spend all those 10 months in the gym; you were distracted by your postgrad studies and other things not related to sports."

"Major, Sir, I don't know how to answer without descending into mysticism. I can only say that asteroid fever fundamentally changed me. My intense desire to live must have affected my psyche, even my brain, creating new neural connections, apparently in great numbers. You've seen the diplomas in my file. How could an ordinary home boy without much talent do that in such short time? Something snapped in my brain, or vice-versa; perhaps it was repaired. I began to read faster, to better retain new information, to instantly identify essential issues amid a flood of words. In general, I changed, and I guess my motor skills also changed."

"You haven't convinced me, Cadet. You won't say anything else, will you?"

"I don't have anything else to say, Sir. I've often surprised myself in the past year."

"OK, Lavroff, I'm not a federal security officer. I believe you. Let's leave this for now. I need you for something else. You don't look like the fighter that you really are. I want to show the senior cadets that an adversary's appearance can easily be misleading; they see themselves as trained commandos. I won't send you to them right away; you might not be able to handle it. I need a clear guaranteed result. In the next few months we'll get you into shape and polish your fighting tactics. Let's begin right now. Put on protective gear; let's make a man of you."

***

The next class unexpectedly turned out to be a test. Our platoon was taken to the auditorium with virtual simulators. At first the exercise task didn't seem original: our regiment was supposed to land on a planet that was occupied by the enemy. The first wave established a foothold and awaited the main force's arrival with heavy equipment. Then it got interesting.

Orbital intelligence reported that the enemy was preparing a powerful rocket and artillery attack on the foothold, and focused its self-propelled artillery and volley launchers there. Our orbital force was busy fighting in space and couldn't help the commandos. Our platoon's goal was as follows: to land in an area not controlled by the enemy's space defense, quickly march to their artillery, then attack and dislodge them, thus thwarting the attack on the troops that had landed.

The task seemed rather odd because there was nothing about protecting the advancing artillery. Also, the quantity and quality of the attacking forces remained unclear. I was also vexed by the lack of data for the enemy's atmospheric aviation activity in the area. This aside, we were told that the top three platoons that completed the task would be the first in our Academy to get city day passes.

We sat in the simulators. Bearing in mind my experience with the Small Dragon, Inga trusted me with the combat robot and thus with piloting my squad's dropship. The electromagnetic catapult sped up the dropship, hurling it towards the planet. The battle in orbit continued and two pursuit planes escorted us to the edge of the atmosphere.

They wouldn't enter the atmosphere since they weren't designed for that. Having smoothly altered their trajectory they faded away in the black sky. The dropship rocked up and down. I noticed that the radar screen showed Inga going into battle on her machine with the first squad. A bit behind me the dropship of the third squad descended; it was commanded by a quiet Hindu man named Jasvinder.

The landing area was shown by an illuminated green grid. So far, there was no hostile activity along our path, but our tactical orientation bothered me with its stupidity. There was serious combat on both the planet and in space, but here, some 300 kilometers from the foothold seized by the attacking side, was just peace and tranquillity.

Well, let's say that enemy space defense in this area had been neutralized by an orbital blow, which made sense because we couldn't let the enemy have long-range weapons in the planned dropship landing area. But the enemy wasn't a fool either. He knew there was a hole in his defense, and this hole can fill with all sorts of vermin. While that was happening - and we were actually those vermin – he, the enemy, sat on his ass doing nothing. Besides, he was bringing artillery and missile launchers right near the boundaries of this 'black hole' and wasn't trying to take control of this area. This just doesn't happen! I didn't believe it!

As a squad commander, I had direct communication with the platoon commander. So, I called Inga.

"Listening to you, Com-2," she answered tensely.

"Any new information about enemy activity in the landing zone and above it?"

"No new info. Our scanners don't see anything suspicious either. Why are you fidgeting and distracting me?"

"We left the transport ship 15 minutes ago, and in modern combat everything can change 10 times during that time. The enemy must have certainly taken measures to restore its space defense. At the very least mobile launchers can be there. And aviation could arrive as well."

"Stop stirring things up. Our scanners are clear; we weren't told of any changes. Continue descending and stop pestering me," angrily said Inga and cut off.

We were more than halfway now. Apparently, serious anti-space defenses in the vicinity of the landing area had been neutralized by our orbital blows, but now we were in range of mobile anti-aircraft defense systems that could pound us with a dozen surface-to-air missiles. Small Dragons would soon be able to hit us with their backpack-launched missiles.

Well Inga, do as you please, but I won't foolishly go into uncharted territory. Three imitators slipped out from under the bottom of my dropship. They quickly dispersed, taking up positions just ahead: on the right, on the left and below, diligently posing as dropships at all wavelengths. I launched two missiles with electronic warfare stations in its capsule, as well as an unmanned recon aerial vehicle equipped with a powerful scanner. The URAV immediately sped to the planet. The EW missiles sped forward and then turned round, and started flying big circles around the dropship in opposite directions.

"What are you doing, Com-2?" I heard the platoon commander's indignant voice in the headphones of my helmet.

"Take measures to protect the dropship when entering a zone of possible enemy resistance," I quoted the field manual.

"But you were told that the landing zone was safe..."

"Commander," I interrupted Inga quite sharply, "in battle everything changes within minutes. The information we got long ago is now outdated..."

I was cut off by a howl of the siren. The URAV had descended low enough to break the enemy EW's protective umbrellas with the rays of its scanner. Aware that he was detected the enemy started to act.

"There's a missile salvo from the ground!" the voice of third squad commander, Jasvinder, could be heard in the communication channel.

Hypersonic missiles quickly closed in. The first squad dropship flew at the front of the group, making it an excellent target. Inga released radio-locating and thermal traps, but they didn't do much good at that distance. Missiles had already locked in onto their target and held tight. The platoon commander tried to dodge the first and almost succeeded, but it exploded about 30 meters away. A hail of debris showered the dropship, which is bulky and clumsy due to its heavy armor, and because of that it can't maneuver as a fighter. If that had been all, then Inga could have landed the damaged ship, but the second missile gave her no such chance. About 500 meters ahead of my dropship a fireball swelled up: it was a direct hit. Exactly one third of our platoon, with the commander, ceased to exist.

Having lost the best and nearest target, the rest of the missiles tried to redirect to the other ships. Two tore my imitators to shreds, which didn't even try to set decoys and take evasive action. The remainder went after the third squad's dropship. I was saved from being detected thanks to the electromagnetic suppression system of the EW missiles that I sent ahead in good time. Having seen the unenviable fate of the first squad, Jasvinder immediately repeated what I had done. But it was late, and now his destiny depended largely on chance. I couldn't let myself be distracted by him – my dropship was heading directly toward the enemy's staunch defense, and something had to be done urgently.

When the commander was killed with the first squad, I automatically became platoon leader, which means that the company's communications also passed to me. I asked for an orbital strike, but received a categorical rejection. All fleet forces focused on maintaining safe passage for the transport of heavy weapons and the second wave of troops to the foothold.

All I had was two sub-wing launchers with unguided rockets, 20 pieces in each. On the screen I saw the enemy missile launch sites, which were glowing red dots. I turned the dropship's prow a bit and tilted it forward, then let the computer aim the rockets at the target and confirmed the launch. The unguided rockets rushed to the ground, leaving straight fiery red strokes behind. Dropship rockets were usually equipped with thermobaric warheads, which covered quite a large area and cleared the enemy from the area needed for landing. Those waiting for us below would end up battered by this unpleasant surprise. Following my salvo of rockets, to my joy the landing site was hit by rockets from the third squad dropship. It turned out that Jasvinder was still alive and in the fight. Now, only the heavy equipment below, such as tanks or large combat robots, could escape destruction. If we'd face a meeting like this on the landing, we wouldn't stand a chance. I hoped it wouldn't happen. After all, this was just training and there was no point in giving cadets impossible tasks.

There were neither tanks nor heavy robots down there, and at that moment I realized we wouldn't be able to accomplish the task, at least not in full. After landing, we discovered the charred debris of five enemy light robots. For the most part, all we needed to use on them was a set of unguided rockets from one dropship. But we had thrown everything we had at them, and besides, we lost one dropship with unguided rockets equipped with thermobaric warheads that we badly needed. What would we use against the quarg's self-propelled cannons and launchers – it was a very unsettling question.

Nonetheless, our mission wasn't over and we remained in the simulators. Our superiors still wanted to see what we'd do next, and we energetically began to satisfy their interest. We left our dropships on the landing site. One was damaged but still capable of flying, although not as fast as we'd like. In terms of weapons and ammo, the dropships only had aircraft guns and one disposable unmanned recon aerial vehicle on the third squad's damaged dropship. In my plan, the dropships had a rather important role to play, but for now we didn't need them.

I didn't like the idea of a quick march in an unknown and unexplored area, but our mission didn't offer any other options. Of course, we could use the last disposable URAV, but I needed it for my plan's last phase. On the other hand, it wasn't much use in this case. Basically, it was an unguided rocket equipped with a camera, scanner and a transmitter. The dropship also needed it to do recon for the landing site. One couldn't make it maneuver and find the enemy across a large territory.

I dispatched the main patrol, as well as side patrols from the light infantry. Two men remained in the dropships - one in each, and were told to send them into autonomous flight on my signal, or by a timer if there was no signal. I didn't trust the communication system at all - any kind of dirty tricks could be expected from the enemy's EW systems, or from our instructors, who also might want to mess with our minds. It was better to do everything with our own hands.

Apparently, the exercise's legend showed that the enemy was just as disorganized as we were. After all, when the orbital defense was broken commandos landed at many sites across the planet. In near space orbit the battle for control over low orbits continued; the defenders weren't able to do everything as planned. Our team was discovered twice. The first time we were spotted by three fighters that seemed to have their own mission. After shooting at us from afar, they returned on course and flew in the direction of our foothold.

About 10 minutes later two attack planes appeared that were clearly looking for us, apparently following a lead from the previous guests. We met them with four surface-to-air missiles from the backpack launchers of our two Goanna combat robots. We only shot down one, however. The second aircraft launched a swarm of rockets. Fortunately, only a few turned out to be guided missiles.

Dodging our missiles, the attack aircraft was unable to aim properly and almost all the unguided rockets missed their targets. Nevertheless, the aerial attack cost us five dead commandos and one combat robot that was destroyed with its pilot. The attack aircraft left without risking a second attempt, and we abruptly changed direction and returned to the route 15 minutes later. Judging by the rumbling and flashes to the right, they didn't forget us and tried to blast us with missiles.

My Goanna was now our only remaining relatively heavy weapon, if one could say that about a light combat robot equipped with a a rotary machine-gun, anti-tank grenade launcher and the last surface-to-air missile. We had almost made it, and this was the time to use the URAV and dropships.

The unmanned recon aerial vehicle rustled over our heads, flying low over low-lying trees and leaving an inversion trace in the sky, which appeared as a mark on my tablet. Before the URAV was brought down, it captured the scene unfolding below. We got there just in time. In a spacious clearing in the woods 18 missile launchers on large wheeled platforms were taking up positions. Their launch rails with tactical missiles faced our foothold located 300 kilometers to the north. A bit further, near the forest edge, self-propelled assault cannons pointed their barrels at the sky. For tube artillery 300 kilometers was rather far. If they'd use rocket-propelled shells, then they'd reach it.

The fragile missile launch systems were not left without protection. Our URAV was brought down by mobile air defense missile systems, which I, well more like the Goanna's computer that processed the obtained image, counted to be six. Somewhere in the woods most likely were infantry providing cover with armored vehicles. To deal with all this we only had one light robot, five commandos in heavy armored space suits with anti-tank weapons, and eight guys in light armor with machine-guns and a couple of sniper's rifles; as well as two dropships with empty launchers and a couple of automatic aircraft guns.

As one old song goes: the odds before the fight aren't in our favor, but we'll play. The dropships flew very low, almost touching the treetops, and they slipped off the forest edge unleashing location decoys. They were already detected, of course. The enemy recon drones flew nearby and scanned the area. We could only count on the relative strength of the dropships. I hoped they could deal with a couple of light missile strikes from mobile air defense systems.

In part, the dropships did their job, firing dozens of shells from 40-millimeter automatic guns before turning into burning debris and crashing into the woods. They even managed to hit one of the targets. Before launch a missile is quite vulnerable, and one of the launchers on the eastern edge of the clearing became a fireball, lighting up an entire field of enemy artillery with a bright flash. The shock wave spread across the clearing, knocking over two adjacent launchers, but the missiles didn't explode. The enemy had positioned the launchers wisely, anticipating our possible attack. So, the domino effect didn't materialize.

Thanks to their suicide attack, the dropships gave my small detachment a few precious minutes to make a move. The enemy spotted us but was unable to destroy the rest of the platoon. As a relatively compact group we stormed the protected position opposite the destroyed launcher, where we were least expected. Our target was the self-propelled assault cannons and missile systems.

Only I could hurt them with a little help from my friend Goanna and the heavily armored commandos. Everyone else covered us and diverted the enemy's fire. But the attacking enemy forces had overwhelming numerical superiority. The heavily armored commandos could fire one anti-tank rocket each, but then they were swept away by a hail of shells. I couldn't say much about the guys in light armor; they were able to give us 15 seconds at most. I was left alone very quickly. There were six anti-tank missiles with cumulative warheads in my Goannna's left manipulator cylinder, awaiting just the right moment.

I targeted a couple of self-propelled assault cannons and four missile systems, and gave the computer the command to fire when ready. Missile homing heads took some time to aim, and I tried to buy time. I jumped into the enemy position, trying to knock off anyone armed with light weapons. I didn't shoot, but instead relied on my armor and mobility. I was hoping the enemy wouldn't use heavy weapons for fear of hitting their own guys. But I was wrong.

In fact, that's how it was for the first five seconds; the enemy was rather confused. But after the launch of my very first missile aimed at a self-propelled assault cannon about to fire, the enemy's priorities changed instantly. They shot at me with everything they had. I was hopping about like a frantic hare not giving my own targeting systems a chance to aim, and then I shot all over the place with rotary machine-gun bursts. Its caliber wasn't enough to pierce armored vehicles, but it got the better of infantry body armor, sweeping away attached implements and outer sensors of scanners on even heavily armored vehicles.

In the 10 seconds that I had won, Goanna's computer fired three missiles. I saw the first hit the target: a 200-millimeter self-propelled assault cannon turned into a flaming bubble and exploded, scattering pieces of armor and gun fragments. Then I got hit by something serious.

The light darkened for a moment and there was the familiar report of exit from virtual reality. The exercise was over.

My fellow squad comrades had already exited their simulators and watched my combat on the big screen on the auditorium wall. When I appeared, Inga stood up and reported completion of the 17th platoon's training to the professor, Colonel Gustafsson, a gray-haired man with a Scandinavian appearance.

The Colonel also stood up.

"Platoon, attention! Cadets, the computer evaluates the execution of your unit's task as a conditional success. You failed to disorganize the enemy and to prevent a rocket-artillery strike on the foothold, but you delayed the attack and reduced the enemy's strength to the point that air-defense units of our troops that landed were able to prevail. You made up for your gross error during landing by taking the correct actions afterward. The platoon as a whole passed the test, and each cadet will be sent a complete review of his actions during the task, as well as his own grades. Not all of you passed. I'll tell you right away that the death of the entire unit on a mission will be a minus to your overall assessment. Your place among all first-year training platoons will be announced in the evening."

We finished second. The fifth platoon won because after completing their task seven cadets managed to retreat to the forest and escape pursuit. They also couldn't stop the attack completely, but weakened it considerably as we had done. The commander of the fifth platoon was my nemesis, Stephen Fulton.

Chapter 7

Our officers didn't let us down, and next Sunday we got a leave of absence to go to town. That Saturday evening at dinner Inga sat at my table.

"Do you mind?" she asked, putting her dishes with all sorts of fine foods onto the table. Academy meals for future officers were quite generous, and the kitchen delighted us with a wide variety of dishes.

"Not at all, have a seat," I responded in a neutral, friendly tone. Still, Inga was in the company with Steven and Chen, and after that conversation with Chen in the dormitory I didn't know what to expect from her. So, I let her begin to talk.

"You're from Titan, aren't you?" she suddenly asked.

"Yes. I was born and lived there before the Academy."

"Have you ever been to Ganymede before?"

"No, my first time here was when I enrolled."

"So, you know nothing here. I grew up here. Are you going on leave?"

"Sure. I need a change of scenery."

"If you want, I can show you the city. There's a couple of really interesting places that you can't possibly reach by yourself."

Inga puzzled me with her offer. I can't say I didn't like her, but a new conflict with Stephen was never part of my plan. I didn't want to hurt a girl with rejection either, so I thought I'd just ask her outright.

"Inga, will Stephen be furious to know that you're giving me a tour of the city?"

"Stephen? Well, he probably will. But he's not my boyfriend. So, that's his problem. Are you afraid of his rage?" she smiled, but there was clearly interest behind the smile.

"The words 'I'm afraid' aren't appropriate here. I don't care much for Stephen, but there's a reason why I'm here, and I will take into account anything that might interfere with achieving it. If Steven starts a fight the consequences could be tragic. He'll probably get away with it, but no one will stand up for me."

"And because of those fears you'll turn down the girl who asked you to join her?"

Inga clearly was prodding me, and I couldn't figure out why she was doing this, but I didn't think Steven sent her looking for a reason to fight. That would have been too complex for him, and Inga would hardly agree.

"I won't say No," I relented. "But please keep in mind what I said about Stephen."

"I won't tell him anything," Inga smiled triumphantly. "See you tomorrow. At 10 sharp, in the parking lot. Will you come?"

"Most certainly" I also allowed myself a smile.

***

We flew somewhere out of town. From above, a vast wooded plain opened before us. After terraforming, Ganymede resembled the Earth as it was before the Industrial Revolution and the advent of technology, but as it turned out the Solar system's largest moon still preserved something unique. Inga brought me to just such a place. The forest-covered flat hill descended to a small lake. One of its shores was high and steep, overlooking the water by a dozen meters.

"Do you see that precipice?" asked Inga pointing at the opposite bank, "this is Ganymede's original rock which emerges on the surface. It was left untouched for a reason. This moon's crust was once a mixture of silicate rock and ice water. During terraforming, the ice melted, forming extensive branched caves. Now this is a favorite destination for speleologists."

"When I recently was in the office of the Academy director I ran into a female candidate who was also into speleology. It seems her last name is Yakovleva. Did you meet her?"

"We've met before, I think, but a long time ago."

"Shall we go into the cave?"

"Well, if you're not afraid," Inga smiled.

"I never tried it before. I think it's going to be fun."

"Then get the gear out of the trunk; we need to change. We're not going underground in these clothes."

The cave's dark beauty made a strong impression on me. The bizarre vaults cast grotesque shadows in the light of our powerful lanterns. I felt like I was inside a giant petrified sponge. The three-dimensional labyrinth had no floor. The passages went vertically downwards as often as they went sideways or upwards. It was impossible to walk through this cave calmly. We either had to go down or go up with the help of special equipment.

I was covered with sweat under thick overalls despite the fact that the temperature in the cave hardly exceeded 10 degrees Celsius. I couldn't say I was really excited about this, but it wasn't boring. The only place that truly impressed me with its beauty came at the very end. It seemed Inga specifically led me here. The surface of the small underground lake was shiny red, almost crimson in the light of our lanterns. The cave walls were full of mica or something like it: sparkling and splitting the light that fell upon them into thousands of small rays.

"A whole bouquet of minerals has dissolved in the water, but it owes its color mostly to micro-organisms. Rumor has it that these are endemic, but of course that's crazy," Inga smiled. "How do you like it here?"

"It's beautiful. Thank you for bringing me here. It's like a fairy tale."

"You know, I wanted to apologize for yelling at you that day and not listening. In the end, we almost failed."

"Never mind. That's what it's for - in training combat you die virtually, not really. I'm not without sin either. I abused my power and acted without order."

"But you were actually right, and that changes a lot."

"Don't beat a dead horse. It ended well, didn't it?"

"OK. Well then, shall we go back?"

"Let's just stay here a few more minutes. I've never seen such exotic beauty," I responded, outlining the cave roof with a lantern beam.

"I'm glad you appreciate it," I felt Inga's hand on my shoulder and I turned to her.

Two seconds later we were kissing. I enjoyed the taste of Inga's lips and the passion awakening in her. She broke away from me and said in a slightly wheezy voice: "It's possible to swim in the lake. Oddly enough, the water is warm," she took off her clothes slowly, allowing me to examine her in detail, as she plunged into the red lake, "Jupiter warms the insides of its moons with gravitational tides."

"Well, he came up with something really good," I replied also plunging into the water next to her, pulling her strong, flexible body close to mine.

***

They were waiting at the entrance to the cave. The four of them: Stephen, Chen and two more guys from the fifth platoon whose names I didn't know.

"Who do I see, but Inga!" said Stephen, blatantly ignoring me, "You are so incredibly predictable, baby. I knew you'd bring him here."

"Stephen," responded Inga with irritation. She clearly was annoyed that the wonderful time together was now irreparably damaged. "Don't you think it's not a good idea to follow me, to put it mildly?"

"Why not? It's a very good idea. Such a secluded place, your rootless friend and I can discuss all our problems here so that no one interrupts us," said Stephen with a smirk. "You're not gonna make us chase you, right, Cadet Lavroff?"

"Stephen," I spoke with maximum indifference in my voice, "Would you just explain what you want me to do? Maybe I can help without all the nonsense?"

"You? Help me?" Stephen laughed angrily. "Because of you and people like you, my friend, the son of a fifth generation officer, wasn't accepted into the Academy. You're not even fit to shine his shoes! And you're asking how can you help me? Well, fall into the ground or something... Just vanish so that no one in the Academy will even think about you."

"And you want to solve this problem with a little help from your friends?"

"Cockroaches and other pests must be crushed before they breed. And now we're going to make you understand that you're a cockroach and you'd better crawl behind the baseboard. And if you don't understand we'll continue to explain until the fog clears in your stupid head," Stephen took a step forward.

"Stephen, if you lay a finger on him…" Inga hissed, trying to stand in his way.

"Oh, Inga, are you afraid your boy can't solve his own problems and will wet his pants? Just get out of the way while I'm still asking nicely, okay?" Stephen was clearly losing control of himself.

It was time to step in.

"Wait guys. I got a better idea" I said as calmly as possible looking into Stephen's eyes. "You want me to write a letter of resignation, am I right?"

"Oh! Has your brain finally awoken?" asked Stephen mockingly.

"Fine," I continued, completely disregarding his tone. "Then why all this fuss? If we fight here there's a chance the consequences will impact our future studies including possible expulsion from the Academy. None of us need that. As for you, Stephen, your Dad will cover your back, but I'm not sure about your friends."

Chen's eyes and those of his friends were for a moment filled with doubt. It looked like they weren't sure either.

"Hold on, Stephen, let me finish." I interrupted my opponent who was going to say something nasty with a hand gesture. "I have a better option. Let's go peacefully to our fly-cars and head back to the Academy. The martial arts gym is open 24 hours. We have free time until 8 p.m. and no one will stop us going there. Let's put on protective gear and have a fight. Myself against the four of you. If you win, I'll write a request to the Academy director asking to expel me. But if I win, then you write that request. About the rest of you, I don't care."

For a moment Stephen hesitated. He wasn't stupid, after all. Such a proposal made him suspicious: this was too easy. But to refuse was beyond his strength, because he'd certainly be considered a wuss. How could these four be afraid to go up against the one who they just verbally abused.

"How do I know that you'll write the expulsion request?" said Stephen, trying to find a loophole.

"Let's make a bet and put the terms on our web pages with our digital signatures. If someone breaks his word, then we know what everyone will think of him."

"Okay, boy. Let's do it. It was your suggestion," Stephen muttered between his teeth while taking out his tablet. "Come here, everybody, I need your signatures.

***

"Why did you do that?" asked Inga in a slightly twitchy voice when the door of her fly-car closed us off from the evil-smirking Stephen and his buddies. Only Chen didn't smile and seemed brooding.

"Don't worry, it'll be fine," I calmly answered, though in my heart I wasn't quite sure. Strangely enough, the guy who worried me the most was Chen, but I dispelled my dark thoughts.

"You're going to beat them in a training fight, one against four? Who are you, Master Lee Chang? Or Ilya Proskuroff?"

"No Inga, I'm not Lee Chang, nor Proskuroff. But I learned from them. From both."

Inga silently nodded and didn't ask any more questions about the upcoming fight.

***

As expected, the martial arts gym was empty on a weekend afternoon. Having put on our protective gear, we entered the ring and went to the referee's computer to set the fight terms. The protective gear absorbs most of the force of any strike and keeps the limbs, neck and back from bending at unnatural angles. The fighter doesn't feel much pain and is safe from fractures. Depending on the point at which the impact occurs, however, the gear loses flexibility and simulates the consequences of the damage inflicted; sometimes temporarily and sometimes for the whole fight. For example, a severe blow to the head or to the liver might lead to total paralysis that simulates a knockout or knockdown.

Once, I asked Major Steinitz why we didn't use such gear for the entrance test. He explained it's good for perfecting fighting skills, but if protecting a fighter it greatly distorts his perception of the fight's reality and doesn't allow an instructor to correctly assess a candidate's psychological condition during the match.

Inga stood alone outside the combat area looking at me. Suddenly, the front door opened and a crowd of cadets burst in.

"Hi guys," shouted a short man with a third-class chevron walking first through the door. "You're going to have a big party here. Why'd you send invitations out so late? You could have earlier put the terms online. We barely made it."

"Holy shit," Chen quietly swore, but I heard it.

The crowd grew larger and a thick ring formed around the fight area. I thought maybe it was for the best. Steven can't go back now, and the same for me.

The referee's computer gave a 30-second alert. We went to opposite sides of the ring and faced each other. The transparent walls that closed the ring's border descended from above, forming a sort of hexagonal aquarium in which we were the fish. According to the terms we had chosen only a knocked out fighter left the ring, but no restrictions were placed on use of fighting techniques, up to the point until it was allowed to finish off a fighter who was down. The fight time was not limited and would end only with victory for one of us.

The starting bell sounded and two of my opponents scattered, flanking me. I didn't try to stop them. Stephen and Chen were directly in front. While I didn't know their level of training I could guess that they had been taught well in the Australian Mobile Infantry School. Out of the corner of my eye I noticed a sharp move by the opponent on my right. I didn't dodge or block his blow but made a counter move at an acute angle to his impact, instantly shortening the distance. The enemy's fist slipped tangentially over my head, followed by a second-hand blow to the liver. I dodged it slightly, changing my body trajectory. The distance became so short that it was hard to punch and I used my favorite elbow blow. While I had hit Major Steinitz in the shoulder my current opponent, whose name I didn't even know, was struck hard under his chin.

I remembered that behind me was an adversary whom I hadn't seen for a few seconds and I didn't know what he was doing. Anticipating a worst-case scenario, I moved right with a jump and a roll-over in the direction of the one part of the ring where my opponents were definitely not. As it turned out, good thing I did.

The opponent who outflanked me on the left thought I was going to counterattack his friend on the right, recklessly making myself a target. He gathered momentum in two steps and with a classic jump across half the ring he slammed me in the back with a straight kick. My back, however, was already flying in a totally different direction with the rest of my body. The powerful blow that should have knocked me out instead landed in my opponent who was crippled by my elbow.

As a result of these moves my opponents set up a triangle whose base was formed by Chen and Stephen, who only had just begun to move. In the vertex of the triangle facing me, my third nameless opponent, still slightly stunned, was standing. I wasn't going to give him time to recover. Having made some feints, I provoked him to counterattack with his foot. His leg was starting to straighten, but I had already moved forward and sideways, going behind my opponent and giving him a chop at the base of the skull. My opponent cringed and fell forward, but I had to avoid a sudden blow to the face which Chen made at enviable speed. It was a nasty strike, with the fingers and palm open. Compared to the punch this blow was seven inches longer and was an unpleasant surprise. I only knew this technique theoretically and had never seen anyone hit like that in a real fight. I could do nothing but lean backwards, and that was clearly not the best defense since it upset my own equilibrium, leaving me in an unstable stance.

I had no doubt that Chen and Stephen would try to take advantage of this, so I jumped backwards moving into the air like a cat and going into a long roll. I had enough space behind me, and I didn't crash into the ring's transparent wall. But a second later it turned out that I couldn't put enough distance between us. I was barely on my feet when Chen and Stephen attacked from both sides. They never got around me, but a simultaneous attack by two well-trained opponents can end badly for the person attacked. It was probably not the first time they fought together. At least they attacked at different levels and didn't interfere with each other.

Chen kicked my left thigh, and Stephen attacked with a double punch to my head while jumping. It turned out that I had nowhere to step back because the last time I jumped I used all the distance to the edge of the ring, and I couldn't duck to the right or left because my opponents attacked in these directions. I jumped forward and up, leaving the line of attack of both opponents.

At the same time, I kicked my foot into the liver of Stephen, who outflanked me from the right. Sprawling in the air I tried to punch Chen's head who was trying to break the distance. Chen dodged the blow, but Stephen was hurt pretty bad. The leap he made trying to punch me in the head literally put my opponent in the way of my counterstrike. The referee's computer considered that my kick knocked Stephen out and signaled the withdrawal of the third person from the fight.

I landed quite nicely, but swayed at once. My left hip was numb; it looked like Chen's kick finally hit its target. He also figured it out and didn't give me time to recover. He competently closed the distance, trying to approach from the side of my injured leg, but now he was alone and I had no more distractions. I tried to keep my opponent from closing the distance by moving fast and making false threats with the deceitful movements of my hands and feet. With each passing second I felt that my left leg was getting better. Apparently, from the computer's point of view, the force of Chen's hit was not enough to cause serious injury.

The crowd behind the transparent walls roared like a wounded mammoth, but by this time nothing could spoil my fighting spirit. I felt like I caught the wave and now

Chen didn't stand a chance. It looked like my adversary felt something like that. In any case, he was no longer going forward, closely following my actions and evidently planning to meet my attack with a carefully prepared trick. I didn't disappoint him. As soon as my leg finally returned to normal, I jumped forward. Chen was even better prepared than I thought. He reacted to the very start of my jump, was able to correctly estimate its trajectory and shifted slightly aside, simultaneously moving towards me and preparing to meet me in the air. But he thought I was gonna hit him in the head or the body, and I didn't hit him at all.

I waited for his kick. When he moved his leg sharply ahead, aiming at my stomach, I hit his kneecap with my fist. Thanks to my hand's movement, while striking Chen my body was turned in the air and and his foot didn't hit me. When I landed Chen finally got me with a sensitive punch to the jaw, which I partially evaded, but it didn't matter much. My head returned to normal in five seconds and the critical knee injury prevented Chen from taking advantage of this. Then the fight ended almost instantly: an approach from the side of the injured leg, a false movement, an ankle trip and the finishing knee-stab to the body. It seemed Chen wasn't seriously fighting anymore, but merely showing that he'd fight to the end.

The audience roared enthusiastically, enjoying the unexpected free entertainment. In the first row near Inga I saw Major Steinitz who looked at me closely. He smiled when his eyes met mine, slowly moving his palms three times, to indicate applauding. He then nodded and walked through a crowd of cadets to the door.

* * *

To his credit Stephen began writing the expulsion letter from the Academy before even leaving the gym. He stripped his gear off and threw it, then grabbing his tablet and typing on a virtual keyboard in a frenzy. His comrades shuffled awkwardly a few steps away, but nobody tried to get involved. In a few minutes Steven finished writing and was prepared to click on the send icon.

"Stephen," I stopped him at the last minute, approaching the group of my recent opponents, "can we talk?"

"What do we have to talk about, Cadet Lavroff?" said Stephen in a surprisingly calm voice. You won. Isn't it enough or do you want to savor the triumph and watch as I send the Academy director a letter that will ruin my career? Well, I don't care anymore," and he put his finger over the icon with a stylized arrow.

"Don't rush, Cadet Fulton," I said, touching his hand. "Didn't you read the bet terms carefully?"

"I read it carefully enough to know it's better not to avoid fulfilling the conditions. I wanted to check if you'd bolt in case of a loss, and I read the entire text."

"There is a deferral clause that the winner may choose to grant to the loser."

"Yes, there is. You want to give me a break after everything that's happened between us?" asked Stephen with a bitter grin.

"I'm ready to do it," I answered, looking at him in the eye after he raised his head. "You're a good cadet and could be a good officer in the long run, if only you'd do something about your character. I never forget that the Federation is waging a difficult war, and I don't want the army to lose a fine and motivated officer. I'll defer the lost bet until Academy graduation. But I have one condition."

"And what am I supposed to do?" Stephen seemed confused.

"Nothing. Nothing at all. Leave me alone for good and don't stop Inga from socializing with me if she wants. That also goes for your friends. How you convince them - that's your problem."

"Is that all?" Stephen asked gloomily, but his voice trembled treacherously.

"That's all I need from you. Do you accept?"

"Yes."

"Well, good luck here; I've things to do," I turned and started to leave.

I was 10 paces away when Stephen's voice caught up with me: "Lavroff!"

"What?" I turned to him.

"Thank you. I can't imagine my life without the army."

"Thank the quargs. Best with a large-caliber cannon."

***

The next day saw two notable events. In the morning I was called to the Academy director instead of training with Major Steinitz. I thought this was connected to yesterday's incident, but the conversation turned out to be completely different.

Major Ignatoff was in Lt. General Shiller's office in addition to the General himself. I reported and, miraculously, was seated at the conference table.

"Cadet Lavroff," began Shiller. "Major Ignatoff conveyed your views about creating a course on the use of weapons and equipment captured from the quargs. It's a good idea and I discussed it with the Academy Board of Trustees, who are people with bigger stars on their shoulders than I. They liked it. In a week the Academy will get some captured robots, hand-held weapons and armored space suits. Our task is, first, to make usable the weapons and equipment; second, to train the Academy's technicians in hacking the enemy equipment and its maintenance; third, to develop and launch a program to train third-year cadets in mastering this equipment and weapons. Any questions and suggestions?"

I looked at the major, but he didn't say anything.

"May I, Lt. General, Sir?" I asked and, after an affirmative nod from the General, continued: "The first two items can and should be merged. I've got experience working with Academy technicians in hacking and making the Small Dragon ready for battle. They know their business well and are happy to learn new things. By the time the first part is finished the second part will have been largely solved."

"Accepted," my assessment of the Academy technicians pleased the General and his spirits improved. "What are your thoughts about the task's third part?"

"There won't be any problem," Major Ignatoff interjected. "Our instructors have enough experience training cadets in mastering Federation equipment and weapons. They'll master the captured equipment pretty quickly. Anyhow, Cadet Lavroff managed to coach me well in just a couple of weeks. Next, we can basically rewrite the existing curricula, making the necessary additions, of course."

"Well," the General was evidently going to say, 'Officers, sirs', but stopped when he remembered that not everyone was an officer. "Instructors, sirs, I expect you, Major, to prepare a plan for stage three, and you, instructor Lavroff, to develop a technical staff training program and a plan for the first phase. Any questions?"

I looked at the Major again. The situation clearly amused Ignatoff, who was interested in looking at me from the 'outside'.

"Lt. General, Sir," I asked cautiously, "What do these new duties mean in terms of my further training?"

"Cadet Lavroff, you're already exempt from physics and math classes. For other theoretical subjects, except for special subjects, you are allowed free attendance. Exams and tests will be taken individually. As of tomorrow, you'll be an instructor in captured weapons and equipment with an appropriate stipend and all the corresponding duties and rights. Major Ignatoff will explain the details. Congratulations, Cadet, on your new assignment."

"Serving the Earth Federation," I answered, standing at attention, as was the rule.

"That will be all, Sirs. You're free to go."

The night before taps, my tablet received an interstellar call with the backdrop of the Fifth Strike Fleet headquarters of the Earth Federation. A little stunned, I checked if my room door was closed and accepted the incoming call. The backdrop faded with a quiet ring and I saw an admiral in uniform.

"Admiral, Sir…" I automatically jumped up from my chair.

"Stand down, Cadet, my call is unofficial. I'm Admiral James Fulton, deputy chief of the Fifth Strike Fleet headquarters and, at the same time, the father of your fellow student, Stephen Fulton. You know what I want to talk about?"

"I guess so, Admiral, Sir."

"I heard about your conflict," the Admiral paused a little, and I didn't say anything. "I like how gracefully you transformed a vulgar brawl, categorically forbidden by the regulations, into a training combat with a bet. It's a beautiful solution."

"Thank you, Admiral, Sir, I also thought it was good."

"But that's not what I want to talk about. You're 16 now, right? Let's put aside my opinion of how I think you won a fight against four others, even though one of your opponents was a martial arts champion at the Australian Mobile Infantry School. The main thing that surprised me was that you showed rare foresight for your age by giving my son the opportunity to graduate from the Academy."

"Since you know the details, Admiral, Sir, you also know my motives."

"Of course, I do. You taught my son a lesson in honor, Cadet Lavroff, and it did him some good. I thank you for what you've done. I think you'll make a great officer."

"Thank you, Admiral, Sir."

"One more thing, Cadet. There's no telling how your fate will turn out. If help is needed, you've got my direct contact information in your tablet."

The device vibrated, indicating an incoming message.

Chapter 8

Four months later we were told of the first major exercise, which included a genuine planet landing. All the first-year cadets, along with equipment, weapons and ammo, were loaded into the transport ship, *Macedonia*, which was assigned to the Academy, and sent to the Leiten star system. In addition to a pair of giant gas planets and three asteroid belts, the system had an Earth-like planet that could support human life. Leiten-5 previously led an unremarkable existence as an unwelcome cold stone ball full of ice. A small artificial sun placed in its orbit transformed the planet, however, and recent terraforming made its atmosphere breathable. Much still had to be done in order to adapt Leiten-5 to human colonization, but the planet was still a perfect testing ground for commandos.

Apart from myself, whose status had so far been transitional and unclear for both cadets and Academy staff, our group consisted of five instructors, including Major Ignatoff. General Schiller appointed our tactics professor, Colonel Gustafsson, as senior officer. All junior commands were held by cadets, assigned as platoon and squad commanders based on the simulator test results. Inga kept her position as our platoon commander despite failing the first test. I was relieved from the Com-2 position in order to assume my new duties.

In addition, we had a technical team for the captured weapons and equipment that we got up and running in the past four months. One of our tasks was to learn how to handle these in combat conditions. Also, the academy director found it useful to scare first-year cadets with real enemy combat equipment.

Just in case, the outdated corvette, *Impetuous-1415*, served as our escort. After leaving Ganymede's orbit, we accelerated and jumped into hyperspace. Earth Federation's science didn't yet know about stationary hyperportals, so we traveled to the Leiten system via a series of linear jumps that took almost a week. The ship had plenty of space for training and it could easily hold three times as many commandos, so the instructors didn't let us get bored.

Before the last jump in the long chain, Colonel Gustafsson gathered the officers for a meeting in the *Macedonia's* bridge to finalize matters for the upcoming exercise. This decision turned out to be fatal for the officers. As we emerged from hyperspace, 400,000 kilometers from Leiten-5, which was our destination, we found ourselves in the thick of a battle. While we were in hyperspace the quargs launched a surprise attack on the Leiten star system and were storming Leiten-5.

A nearly unarmed transport ship escorted by a dilapidated corvette that appeared out of subspace was a gift to the quargs. The corvette was immediately pounded by an enemy cruiser, and burst into flames and fell apart. Only a few randomly spinning fragments remained. The *Macedonia* was also battered. Of course, we didn't see any of this since we were in the ship, but we felt the full extent of it.

Our pilots, aware of the hopelessness of the situation, tried to speed the ship up in the direction of the planet, where the remnants of the Orbital Defense Force tried to withstand the onslaught of an overwhelming enemy force. In part they even succeeded, but the almost simultaneous impact of a heavy shell near the conning tower, as well as a torpedo into the stern, killed the pilots and destroyed the cruise engine. After putting several more shells into the large but almost defenseless ship, which was now immobile and out of control, the quargs left it alone. Apparently, they decided to deal with it later, after the orbital defense had been crushed. The *Macedonia* continued its uncontrollable drift towards the planet, as heavy steam poured from the breaches.

***

The alarm sounded almost simultaneously with the sharp acceleration that threw people to the floor, even though the gravitational compensators were working to their limit. The *Macedonia's* pilots would only make such a sudden maneuver in absolutely desperate circumstances. A strong blow a minute later, followed by another, shook the ship from bow to stern, confirming this conclusion. These were the circumstances we faced. After the second impact, the ship stopped accelerating, and its interior gravity declined sharply to about a third of the norm. It didn't take much intelligence to understand that a powerful enemy ship, and perhaps more than one, had pounded the *Macedonia*.

I got up on my feet and ran to the closet that held my combat space suit. There are advantages as an instructor:

you can keep personal weapons and equipment in your cabin, not in the armory. While I was putting on my suit, the ship was shaken by three more major hits. I tapped into the command network and suddenly heard the monotonous synthesized voice of the ship's computer.

"...attacked by the enemy. The captain and the pilots are dead. Senior officer has to take command of the ship. The ship has been attacked by the enemy."

"This is Cadet Lavroff, an instructor in captured weapons," I shouted without thinking.

"Your authority is confirmed. You're senior; take charge of the ship."

"I assume command. Report the situation."

"The ship has been attacked by the enemy. The conning tower was destroyed, the cruise engine was destroyed, extensive damage to the stern. The reserve control post was destroyed. The chief cabin and mid deck living quarters are partially destroyed and depressurized."

"What are the casualties?"

"All officers and up to one third of cadets are lost."

"Where are we heading?" I continued to ask questions while running along the central corridor towards the armory.

"The ship is drifting uncontrollably. Maintaining speed and direction it will enter Leiten-5's atmosphere in 33 minutes. Considering current damage, landing is impossible. I recommend an escape on dropships as we approach the planet."

"What's happening in space and on the planet?"

"An enemy fleet with 18 battleships is attacking the Leiten-5A orbital fortress. Leiten-5B and Leiten-5C fortresses have been destroyed. I see debris in their orbits. The enemy landed troops on the planet. I have no further information."

"Immediately release access to the armory and start loading equipment into dropships. Turn on general transmission."

"Done."

"Everyone, your attention, please," my voice pealed all over the ship. "This is instructor Lavroff. The quargs attacked our ship during the approach to Leiten-5. All officers were killed when the bridge and conning tower were hit. As the only surviving instructor, I am in command of the ship. The armory has been unlocked. Everyone, immediately get your gear according to the combat plan. Load the equipment and take your seats in the dropships. Platoon commanders: report casualties and load as you connect to the command network.

Technicians: get into dropships 35 to 37 with all equipment, captured combat machines and ammo. Everyone be ready to land on the planet at my command."

I cut off the transmission and called the ship's computer again: "Ship, is there contact with the orbital fortress?"

"Contact established. Speak."

"Leiten-5A, this is the *Macedonia*, a training and transport ship. Instructor Lavroff is in command after all senior officers were killed. Asking for instructions."

"This is Admiral Petroff, commander of orbital defense, or rather of the ruins of the only remaining orbital fortress. *Macedonia*, you're drifting to the planet. In some 10-15 minutes release the dropships and land on the surface. We'll try to distract the quargs, but we won't last long."

"What awaits us on the planet, Admiral, Sir?" I shouted running into the armory, from which there was a continuous stream of cadets in armored space suits and walking tanks, eh, combat robots.

"Actually, nothing good, instructor. There's no answer from there. At least six quarg divisions with heavy armored vehicles landed on Leiten-5. You'll be the only unit on the planet that's remained intact and with some fighting capability. Here's a map that shows the situation at the time when we lost contact with the last unit. I see that your ship isn't in good shape. How many casualties so far?"

"Basically all the commanding officers and about one third of the cadets."

"Try to hold on until the approach of our forces, they won't take too long. The attack on Leiten-5 is a reckless gamble by the quargs. Our fleet will soon arrive. If you find the remains of our forces, join them to your unit."

"I don't have that authority, Admiral, Sir."

"Here are the orders, instructor; I've confirmed your authority." On the screen of my tablet appeared an icon showing the accepted file. "That's all, prepare for landing. Farewell Lavroff," and the Admiral signed off.

I switched to the command channel and plunged into shouts of platoon commanders giving orders to subordinates and quarreling with each other.

"Calm down, everyone," I barked. "Report readiness for landing and casualties. In order, starting with the first platoon."

"First platoon is finishing loading into the dropship. No casualties. Readiness in three minutes. Cadet Shneyerson reporting."

"Second platoon has finished loading. Casualties include seven men. There's depressurization in the bay. No injuries. The Goanna's damaged; we haven't been able to load it. Cadet Smith reporting."

I ran to my dropship while listening to the reports of platoon commanders, and had a mental picture of a badly beaten commando unit that still had its internal compass. Thanks to their efforts, the Academy instructors were able to train our minds to work properly in an emergency. But this is now, while we're still on board the transport ship and haven't yet plunged into a real battle. I'll see how things go. We still have to get out of here now.

"Ship, calculate the optimum dropship discharge point."

"In 143 seconds. Countdown started."

I jumped into my dropship. There were also two captured Small Dragons and four technicians in it. Besides, boxes of quarg weapons and space suits were tightly fastened to the floor. I was suddenly hit by the thought that the quargs also have no problem calculating the point of optimal discharge of our dropships, and don't want to allow us to land on the planet. Which means they'll have to take their mind off the orbital fortress and shoot down our transport ship.

"Ship! Release the dropships immediately!"

Thrust, acceleration, brief moment of weightlessness and re-acceleration: the dropship ignited its own engines. In front of me, on a tactical projection, I saw the planet and a scattering of marks of the regiment's dropships. Fifty-four out of 80 initially loaded on the transport ship. About 10,000 kilometers to the left, I saw the orbital fortress; the ruins of it. But something still shot out from there. I realized they were trying to cover us. Well, good luck, guys. Unlike us, you don't have dropships. You don't even have escape pods. Maybe there are a couple of small ships, but I don't think they survived the slaughter.

There was a bright flash behind our backs. The *Macedonia* ceased to exist. I looked at my watch. The quargs were precise like clockmakers. They burned the ship 15 seconds before the moment of optimal dropship discharge.

"All ships, disengage de-boosters and put engines at full capacity."

A wave of armored vehicles burst forward, leaving behind their hulls torches by the engines pushed to their limits. But we didn't think about being careful and conserving resources. The faster we dive into the atmosphere, the better our chances of survival. We left the transport a minute sooner than we should, which meant we would be under fire for a minute longer than we should.

Furious that their true prey was slipping away, the quargs fired at us in a frenzy, even forgetting the fortress that kept grumbling limply. The great distance, however, prevented them from firing with accuracy. They easily hit a large, non-maneuvering vehicle, but dropships were small and quick; the distance kept increasing, and the quargs didn't want to get close enough to expose themselves to the rest of the fortress canons.

We lost five more dropships, but I was relieved by the jolting that began when we entered the atmosphere. At least one danger was behind us, but what awaited on the surface was uncertain. We were heading to the planet's dark side. Admiral Petrov's map showed a sea beneath us. After the artificial sun had melted the ice, the planet had plenty of water, covering about a third of the surface. The hologram showed the shore was 50 kilometers north. The quargs apparently hadn't yet reached that area, but was it suitable? We needed mountains, preferably with vast natural caves. In theory, such a planet should have enough caves. I remembered what Inga told me about the origin of Ganymede's caves.

"Platoon 17's commander; get on the line."

"I'm listening, commander," Inga responded immediately.

"Do you remember that cave on Ganymede? We need to find something like that, but larger. Otherwise, we won't find a place to hide. I'm sending you the planet's map. Look for it. Quick. The quargs will soon finish off the last fortress and start shooting at us from orbit."

"Okay, one sec. I'll do a request using that criteria. OK. Got something… Three spots within 500 kilometers have ice mixed with hard rock. One in the mountains. Not too high, but probably with many caves. I just sent you the coordinates."

Over the sea along a wide front flew 49 dropships, changing course by nearly 90 degrees and continuing along the coast. Their destination was 15 minutes away.

"Electronic Warfare complexes on full power. Each platoon release one simulator and send it north-northeast to the continent's interior."

I realized the dropships' electronic warfare systems weren't the camouflage fields that I was used to in my previous life, but they could serve as a substitute in some way, especially if the enemy was far away and wouldn't yet bother with us. Maybe my trick worked, or maybe we just got lucky, but we reached the mountains without incident. This part of the planet had a spring, and based on our latitude there might be vegetation. But it was impossible to see anything in the dark.

"Commander, we're here."

"I see, 17th. Slow down. All dropships scan the ground."

"Commander, we've detected ferruginous soils; nothing but a continuous glow on the scanners," interjected the senior technician from the 35th dropship.

We were cloaked in almost absolute darkness, it was absolutely impenetrable due to the planet's lack of a moon. We were helped by scanners that drew the topography on tactical projections, but they couldn't peer inside the rock.

"Now we must decide a place to land. There's no point in flying much longer," I followed the scanner image closely.

Some 40 seconds later a suitable small valley opened before our eyes. I gave the order, and the dropships descended smoothly onto Leiten-5. The ramps descended, rumbling under our feet and the robots' supports. By accident we found an entrance to a system of underground caverns. The thin vault of the cavity in the planet's crust below the surface couldn't hold the weight of a Goanna. A robot fell five meters to the floor of a small cave amid a stream of stones, earth and the pilot's swear words. After that, things got much easier. Inside the vaults of the underground galleries we turned on the robots' headlights and the shoulder lights of our space suits without worry.

"Commander," Inga was calling. These caves have formed differently, not like on Ganymede. The ice is in horizontal layers; when it melted the water flowed into the foothills, washing away soft rock. That's why it has a convenient system of cavities with vaults based on stone pillars. Except I wouldn't go into very spacious halls. There are not enough stone supports, and landslides are possible."

Soon we found several more exits to the surface. One was the size of a big hangar door, and could simultaneously let a couple of dropships enter. Inga supposed it was one of those places where melted water flowed out of the ground. A small rock visor hung over the exit, making it invisible from the air. By morning all our equipment was underground. I set up sentry posts and an electronic security perimeter; then I told everyone to eat their dry rations and get some sleep. It hadn't been the easiest day, so we needed a good rest.

Later in the evening we had our first expanded military council. I invited commanders of all 25 training platoons, as well as the senior technician, to participate. I planned to form eight companies of three platoons each, and two battalions of four companies each, which would simplify troop control. I didn't, however, know many of my classmates well. Command of a company, especially a battalion, can't be trusted to just anyone who can't handle it.

"Ok, platoon commanders, we've got lots of trouble, but our situation also has its advantages," I began optimistically. "We're alive, no one is wounded, we got a relatively secure base, equipment, weapons and ammo, and most importantly, soldiers who can use it in combat. We also have concentrated food rations that helps us to survive long enough, even though they're almost inedible."

My words were met by crooked smirks.

"There are also disadvantages," I continued. "We have no heavy weapons. Our intelligence capabilities are at a bare minimum and what we have doesn't suit our needs. We have no experience in intelligence and sabotage operations. The enemy doesn't yet control the entire planet, but they'll increase their presence in the near future and start building full-fledged planetary and orbital defenses here. The quargs are no fools, and they can guess that our fleet will soon arrive, and that it's outraged by their insolence. Why are the quargs even here? Forget this question for now; we don't have enough information. Our fleet isn't expected to arrive for a month, if not six weeks. Command will, of course, push the admirals and light a fire under their feet, but such an operation takes time. So, we have several options: First, we can sit here underground, quietly like mice, enjoying the concentrated food and wait for our fleet to rescue us. No one will denounce us for this, but I'll hate looking myself in the mirror my entire life."

I fell silent and looked at my subordinates. Judging by the sour look on their faces, they also didn't think it was a good idea.

"Commander, you said a few options," piped up a scrawny Com-4, a guy with an intelligent face but an unexpected sharp look. Izrael Katzman, I remembered.

"Yes. The second: Admiral Petroff told me about the scattered remnants of the 102nd and 105th Infantry Divisions that were based here, as well as several smaller units, some attached to them or with their own tasks; they might be hiding," that was from the file the admiral sent me with the map. "We can do thorough recon, search for them and bring them here. We can save many trained Federation soldiers and officers who, when the fleet arrives, can rejoin our army. If we decide on this option and succeed, then our actions will surely be recognized."

"But, Commander, you aren't happy with this, are you?" there was a rapacious smile on the lips of Stephen Fulton, platoon-5 commander.

There was a reason why I let him stay in Academy. With his bad temper this guy seems to be ruthless to his enemies.

"Yes, Stephen. The second option is a good one, let's begin with it. But it's not the end; it's the means to create here in the caves a combat-capable strike compound which, when our fleet approaches, will be able to capture a foothold and provide the landing party with a safe landing route. Thus, we'll prevent the death of thousands of commandos and greatly reduce the loss of equipment."

My shocked subordinates remained silent.

"Commander," carefully said the senior technician. "We need heavy machinery, robots such as Bison. Only they have weapons that can reach low orbit. Or maybe specialized anti-space defense systems. Again, how to do this without aviation, I have no idea. We don't have enough forces to do this. We'd need a heavy infantry regiment, strongly reinforced by air defenses and the same Bisons."

"I fully agree with the need for such forces," I nodded. "So we're going to use this time to prepare. We're two full battalions, almost a regiment of commandos. We need soldiers from the remaining defeated units to solve our lack of manpower. As far as equipment, that's a lot harder, and right now I don't have an answer. The lack of information is astounding, so first we gotta do some good old recon."

***

I remember how our Academy director said that a commando and a saboteur are two different specialties. I had already spent several hours racking my brain over this problem, torturing the tech guys with questions. Our equipment couldn't help with stealth and invisibility. The manufacturer, careful not to increase the weight too much, and worried about costs, didn't think much about camouflage, such as a coating to absorb waves from any detection system, and electronic warfare. So, it was built in the usual manner: The main features were armor, weapons and mobility. After all, we were commandos, not a recon and sabotage group.

The plan that I had in my head was to gather the surviving soldiers. To do that I needed at least one dropship that was equipped in terms of stealth no less than a specialized recon vehicle. So far, as much as I tried with the EW on-board station settings, I couldn't get the result that I wanted.

"Commander," one technician spoke, seeing my torment. "It's not going to work; it's been tried already. I even read an article by two geeks who, instead of one station, tried to shove two into the dropship. One was for the stern, the other for the bow. Camouflage quality was expected to improve as the area covered by the station narrowed. However, an anomalous stripe appeared at the intersection zone, near the mid bulkhead, and it glowed like a beacon signal in all ranges. They tried to correct it. Each has 12 customizable parameters, and if there are two stations then the number of parameters increases to 144 because each depends on 12 of the other. They've been at it for almost a week, waiting for the computer to optimize the calculations. The stripe was removed, but if the dropship is even slightly damaged then the stripe appears again, and instead of a well-disguised vehicle it glows like a Christmas tree in all wavelengths. So they gave up."

"Stop! We're not going to fight on this dropship. We just have to fly from point A to point B. Do you still have that article?"

"Yes, it was on my tablet. I'll look for it."

After I got the article, I slipped out of reality for a few hours, trying to use this simple idea to find a solution out of completely unsuitable raw material. The tech guys didn't interfere and shielded me from any platoon leaders trying to reach me, explaining that I was meditating on plans for the upcoming campaign. I was grateful to them for that. Two hours later, I finished torturing the virtual keyboard and reconvened the technical staff.

"All right guys, let's carefully remove the EW stations from the three most worn dropships and drag them to my command module. Here's a diagram of how and where we'll install these stations." Then I turned to the senior technician: "Jeff, do you have anything that's more effective than a dropship's flight computer?"

"I'll find something, Commander, but it's not a supercomputer."

"Well, bring it here. I'll draw a diagram for its interconnection."

"Commander, may I ask what will it be?"

"It'll be a dropship that surpasses a scout's combat vehicle in terms of stealth. According to my calculations, by 150 percent."

"But this is impossible. You read the article, Commander. Those guys with two stations couldn't solve the problem after a week, and they had a stationary computer at their university. That thing exceeds the speed of our 'sewing machine' by a few orders of magnitude. And we have four stations here!"

"Besides the computer speed, there's an optimization algorithm. What do you think I did for two hours? I was writing highly specialized software. Let's not waste any more time. Where are my EW stations? Why aren't they here yet?"

The tech guys didn't believe it until the very end. Even after 24 hours of continuous computation, when the computer gave the required group of settings, they remained skeptical. But when we turned on all four stations, and my tech guys looked at the readings, their astonishment was the reward for my hard work.

"Commander, this can't be true," said Jeff with a hoarse voice and pointing his hand to the far end of the cave where my dropship stood. It was no miracle, but the effect was visible even to the naked eye. The dropship's hull was covered with a slight haze and its contours lost their sharpness.

"Hey guy," I said to myself. "You haven't even seen a real camouflage field."

Chapter 9

On our first raid I only took the tech guys and the first squad of my former platoon. And Inga, of course. Her caving experience might be of use. I smiled remembering what the Academy director said about skills not useful for a commando. But one never knows what life will throw at you tomorrow.

We again flew at night. Our target was a site potentially with a cave. For my plan to work we needed a muster point where small groups of soldiers who were connected and mobile could gather. It had to be far from our base to prevent retreating units from bringing the quargs straight to us. We didn't find any caves, but we discovered a network of deep canyons with streams that flowed along the bottom and walls that sometimes hovered at negative angles. This was perfect. We could easily hide from aerial observers and could secretly watch the weak beacon that every five minutes sent a short impulse in a narrow frequency band.

Having equipped the muster point, we flew 200 kilometers inland. The quargs hadn't yet shown any sign of activity in this area. In any case, our scanners didn't spot them. The camouflage was fully operational, so I didn't yet worry for our safety. From this empty and bare rocky plain we launched three small drones with weak transmitters. Low-flying and poorly visible, they scattered in different directions and sent out information packs protected by standard army code that had the muster point coordinates, as well as a message that it was only for 24 hours, and signed by training regiment Commander Lavroff. I didn't mention my status as a cadet in order to avoid unnecessary questions and doubts. I planned to set up similar muster points in a dozen other places. Thanks to our tech guys we had many drones, which are useful for recording and subsequent analysis of cadet actions. They cost nothing and weigh little, so Jeff's boys took many of them.

It took a week to set up our network, carefully covering the area around our base but not getting close. During this time I reorganized the regiment into a two-battalion structure, appointing Inga and Israel Katzman as commanders. Upon closer acquaintance Katzman turned out to be a shrewd young man. I tasked them and the technicians with the daily routine of training cadets to handle captured equipment, as well as combat training. I stayed in control of this and was ready to re-equip another dropship for recon, but then our network finally went off.

On the next scheduled visit to the canyon muster point we got the beacon signal that we were waiting for. I left my dropship in a chosen secluded place, hidden on all sides by the walls of the winding canyon, and from above by a hovering part of the cliff. I took the squad to the beacon, except for a heavy-armored cadet who was left as a guard. As we approached a man in a recon outfit silently separated from the canyon wall. I had never seen such combat space suits, although I knew of their existence and characteristics.

"You're walking loudly, commandos," he said, lifting up his helmet's visor. The guest turned out to be black-skinned, and in the faint morning light we could only see the whites of his eyes. We stopped, looking at the scout.

"Introduce yourself," I said looking into his eyes.

"Captain André Mbia, recon company Commander, 3rd Regiment, 105th Infantry Division. Of the former company, former regiment, former division," he added with bitterness and anger in his voice and looked at me in anticipation.

"Instructor Lavroff, commander of training regiment landing forces, Planetary Commando Academy."

"Do you have a rank, Instructor, Sir?"

"Yes, I do. Except it's not a rank, it's a title with shoulder straps. First-year cadet."

"That's rather unexpected," he grinned.

"Did you reach the muster point alone, Captain?"

"No. My men are a kilometer from here. I'm with one sniper. He's above."

"Do you have a transport ship?"

"A recon fly-car that was left with the main party. What shall we do next, cadet? You invited us here, so if you have something to say, say it."

"We have a base in the mountains. Some 200 kilometers from here. It's a chain of deep caverns. We invite all the remnants of the defeated units to join us."

"200 kilometers? And you walked here?"

"We have a dropship, half a kilometer from here."

Looking clearly surprised, the Captain half-arched his eyebrow.

"A dropship? My scanners didn't pick up anything. Can you show it?"

"Yes, we'll show it, and we'll take you to your people. Follow us, Captain, Sir," I said and turned around, walking up the creek.

We arrived at the base when it was finally dawn. Both machines flew neatly into the entrance hole and descended onto the ground. Fifteen scouts got out of their fly-car at the same time as we did and almost started shooting. Through the high arch of the passageway they saw in the nearby cave a Small Dragon roaming free and maliciously swinging his gun. The sight of an enemy combat robot walking among the commandos shocked them, and I had to yell and wave my hands, shielding the Dragon with my body, until they realized there was no danger.

Then I showed the captain our regiment. He was bewildered by dozens of dropships lined up in even rows as cadets mastered captured weapons under the supervision of technicians. He clearly expected to see something else here.

"Cadet," he asked at last. "Why do scanners detect your dropship far worse than my recon fly-car? In fact, when you look at it, it kind of blurs a little…"

"We upgraded it before the raid: four EW stations now work together."

"And who is your handyman?"

"We have more than one," I said, slightly embellishing.

"You got a pretty good situation here, Cadet. I hope you understand that as an officer and as a higher-ranking soldier, I have to take command of your unit?"

"That's impossible, Captain, Sir."

"I don't understand. Explain."

"Take a look, please," I sent him Admiral Petroff's order.

Mbia studied the document for a minute, then he exhaled with relief, so it seemed to me, and unexpectedly he stood at attention.

"Commander, Sir, 3rd Regiment Recon Company of the 105th Infantry Division with 15 men at your disposal," he reported clearly. My tablet vibrated as it received the command access file to the new unit's communication links.

"At ease, Captain, we're not on a parade ground. Welcome to the Combined Commando Regiment," I extended my hand and he shook it without hesitation.

***

The scouts turned out to be a treasure trove of information. After the defeat of the 105th Infantry Division, the remnants of the 3rd Regiment attempted to retreat into the difficult terrain cut by ravines in the northeast of the continent, but most were destroyed from the air, or forced to surrender. Some, like the Captain and his men, managed to escape and took refuge in a vast network of ravines covered by thick shrubs that covered a large area.

We immediately sent drones there and set up a muster point. The situation was complicated by the fact that the quargs patrolled the airspace and often destroyed our drones. Our network signaled more frequently, however, and the following week our regiment was bolstered by 26 additional soldiers and two officers, all infantrymen from the 105th Division. The 102nd Division fought elsewhere, also in the planet's other hemisphere, but we couldn't yet reach it.

The new fighters' equipment was on its last legs. Some made it to the muster points almost naked, in torn overalls, without armor or weapons. After an exoskeleton dies due to a lack of energy, carrying nearly a ton of armored space suit and integrated weapons becomes nearly impossible.

At the sight of our base the expression of joy didn't fade from the faces of the soldiers and sergeants for several hours. Two weeks of complete uncertainty and pursuit by quarg air patrols had a profound effect on their mental state.

Two officers - a senior lieutenant and a captain - were more restrained. This time I immediately presented them with the Admiral's order. The infantry captain's face showed doubt, but Captain Mbia eschewed any eagerness to insist on his rights when he reported about the results of the raid. The Captain saluted me first and started with the words "Commander, Sir". And that was that.

I placed the senior lieutenant in command of a separate infantry company made up of new recruits. The Captain was offered to be regiment chief of staff, which was not bad for his rank, so he agreed without thinking twice.

Two questions vexed me and kept me awake: where to get heavy weapons, and where did the quargs hold prisoners. I interviewed the new soldiers and officers, but they didn't know much. Surprise attack, alarm, firefights with quarg commandos, loss of command, indiscriminate retreat — That's about all I heard.

Captain Mbia told me more.

"When the quargs destroyed the first orbital fortress it became clear that we wouldn't have to wait long for the arrival of their landing forces. While our troops were deployed to cover the most critical sectors, our company was tasked to cover the area of the upcoming battlefield with recon drones. We went to do that and in an hour three large groups of quarg commandos came down, and more than half of our company went to hell because we had sent drones to more threatened sectors. As a result, no more than a platoon returned to the original position, and it was over within minutes. The enemy didn't even need orbital support; they only used atmospheric aviation. The quargs' advantage proved overwhelming. Now, Commander, you know everything."

"What happened to the drone network?"

"Control of the drones was lost during the defeat of the regimental headquarters. Much of the network was destroyed by the quargs on landing and during their further advance. Some drones must still be operational, but my equipment doesn't have enough power to get through to them."

"What if we hang a transponder near the drone-infested area?"

"It could help. But it will actively radiate, and will be immediately shot down."

"We have a lot of small drones."

"I noticed it," the Captain smiled. "But they can't carry a decent transponder."

"We'll make a chain of three or four indecent transponders."

"Hmm… in theory it might work, but the vulnerability with this idea is very high," said Captain Mbia, with doubt in his voice.

"Let it be. When they shoot down one, we'll send more. If I remember correctly, in case there's no connection to the base module, the recon drones will gather the information, and when the connection is restored they'll send it in one group."

"Have you worked with recon networks before, Commander?"

"No. But I can read."

"That's a useful skill, as it turns out. I have to try," Mbia smiled.

"So, Captain. We'll establish a connection and get the info. Then we'll call off the drones immediately. So, take

Jeff and prepare the technical side of the plan. Will three hours be enough?"

"Yes, Commander."

"Then proceed immediately. We'll begin when it's dark."

***

We got the intel from the drones, but we couldn't recall the transponders. A quarg pursuit plane passed by and the defenseless machines were shredded. Mbia took an hour to analyze the data and then reported to me.

The Captain put his tablet on the table and opened a holographic image of the map of Leiten-5's northern hemisphere. Mbia scaled it up and marked out the area of interest, which was covered by an ample number of red dots.

"These are the remnants of the recon drone network," he explained. "I won't go into detail, but the quarg presence in our part of the planet increases every day. I'll start with space. From the planet surface we see two dozen monitors above Leiten-5. They're trying to replace orbital fortresses that can't be transferred to the captured planet in such a short time. It's not possible to estimate the size of the enemy force, but they have no less than 10 cruiser class ships and above. As far as ground forces, the quargs recalled their landing divisions, replaced by heavy infantry and combat robots. Again, I can't tell you the exact number, but the drones spotted a reinforced division. Plus, their aircraft are constantly in the air."

"Where are they holding the POWs, Captain?"

"There's only indirect intel. The quargs took our equipment they seized to the former site of the 2nd Regiment of the 105th. It's an entire small town with housing, warehouses, equipment depots; everything you usually find at a regiment's base. The few people spotted by the drones were also led or driven in that direction. That makes sense. Why build a POW camp in a field when there are buildings behind good fences that are already suitable for humans. The quargs have enough problems now. But without proper intel, I can't be more specific."

Like us, the quargs don't kill those who surrender, but as far as the fate of these POWs, no one knew. We repeatedly tried to offer a prisoner exchange, but the quargs never cooperated. The enemy evacuated POWs to their interior, and then their trail was lost. No one ever returned. However, sometimes POWs escaped, although that was rare, and it was often with outside help. Those who managed to escape said that they were treated more or less decently in captivity. POWs were not beaten; they were given food, and our medics were able to tend to the wounded if necessary, using available medicines and equipment.

During the past few days no one else came to the muster points, and I decided to end the first phase of the operation, during which the regiment was bolstered by 46 soldiers and three officers, in addition to Captain Mbia's men. For my purposes, this was too few, and the thought of abandoning our fellow soldiers to the enemy was unacceptable. So I asked Mbia: "Captain, can you and your men, under the circumstances, scout the former location of the 2nd Regiment?"

Mbia thought for a moment.

"It depends on what you want to know, Commander."

"The approaches, security, what buildings might hold prisoners, what equipment and in what quantity is on the territory; which quarg units are nearby and can quickly come to their aid in case the camp is attacked…"

"So, there's no need to go inside? It will be enough to scout from the outside?"

"If that's enough to answer my questions, then Yes."

"Then we can do it. But I'd like to ask for your dropship, Commander."

"There's a better option. Jeff and I can upgrade your fly-car within 24 hours just like my dropship. For starters, your EW station is much more powerful. We'll add two that we'll take from the dropships. Your fly-car will be less visible than mine."

"This is great news. Can you do this trick with an armored space suit?"

"In general, yes. But it will be hard to drag even one EW station. We must sacrifice something from either the armor or the weapons. I'll ask Jeff if he has any ideas."

***

Mbia and his men left the night before last. The plan was for them to spend a full day at the site and return by today morning. With many enemy aircraft on patrol above there was no chance of communication. So, I had to wait.

The Captain left for the raid with a 40-hour delay. Jeff was a sharp guy, and he came to me with an idea that I should have thought of. I guess my overexertion had clouded my judgment. I shared with Jeff's Mbia's idea to install EW stations in armored space suits. He immediately remembered the missiles with the EW heads; each dropship had two. I successfully used these missiles in mock battles. How could I forget them? In order to put an EW station into a missile head the designers had to make it compact and light. Sure, this led to less power, but a space suit doesn't need much. Jeff and I, and the rest of the tech guys, dismantled almost half of the dropships' missile stockpile. But the silhouettes of Mbia's men going on the raid blurred slightly before the eyes of those seeing them off.

A whistle came from the cave entrance, and a shadow fell on the floor illuminated by the rays of the rising Leiten star. Captain Mbia's unit was returning to base.

***

As soon as the Captain returned I called a meeting of battalion officers and commanders. Mbia could barely keep up because he was so exhausted. His black face looked gray, but he found the strength to report his findings.

"They're there, Commander, Sir," in front of outsiders Mbia addressed me this way. "Here's the layout of the 2nd Regiment's former location," he continued, as a hologram appeared over the table. "Infantry barracks are here and here. They're holding prisoners. How many, we couldn't figure out. We'd have to get inside to know more. Not too many guards, though. I prepared a detailed report. The main security was an external electronic perimeter, but I don't think that's why there's so few guards. Now, here," Mbia indicated a long low building in the tech park, "and here," his finger moved to the former HQ building, "a large number of heavy robots are deployed, about 30. Mammoths, as well as Large Dragons. They're the quarg army elite. They like comfort and prefer to live in well-built facilities rather than be cooped up in huts. Accordingly, they have about a battalion of infantry combat security and other service units. Our equipment that wasn't totally damaged is stored in the far end of the tech park. We couldn't find out exactly what and how many pieces there are, but 30 kilometers to the west the enemy has an air force of three squadrons. There's enough security. If we make trouble at the 2nd Regiment base they'll be on top of us in three to four minutes."

I looked at the officers' grim faces. None believed that our force could do much. I didn't believe it myself, to be honest. But there was no choice.

"Captain, thank you for your service. Tell your people that HQ thanks them."

"Serving the Earth Federation," answered Mbia listlessly.

"Go to bed now. I don't want to see until morning those who were on the raid."

Mbia saluted and went out, and I turned to the officers.

"Your opinion, Sirs."

"An attack on this viper's nest is certain death," said Captain Minchenko, a tough guy in his 30s with a red face and 10 extra kilos. "If we make a surprise attack we'll kill lots of them, but we won't ever make it out. We'll all die there."

"I don't plan to kill us all by going straight at 'em. Frontal attack is not an option."

"Whether we hit them directly or from the side, the result will be the same," said Captain Lee, a short and smiling Korean in his early 30s who joined us among the last. By the way, he was the only officer with the rank of captain who didn't even think to challenge my right to command the regiment. "Sneaking in quietly is completely unrealistic, wouldn't you agree?"

"Perhaps," I answered, though the thought was still on my mind's edge.

"That means we'll make some noise. Let's say we stealthily focus our forces and launch a surprise attack using rockets with thermobaric warheads. Those quargs who survive will be demoralized. Our prisoners will be fine because they're held in a solid concrete structure with windows sealed by steel flaps. Some quargs are also in barracks and underground structures. The equipment is in boxes and hangars in the tech park. There'll be destruction, but not too much. The next thing you know, the quargs will recover and run for their robots. We'll fight hard of course after breaking into the base with our dropships, Goannas and armored commandos. It'll be a few more minutes, and then some quargs will get to their robots, and this will even out the battle. Then in a minute the quarg air force will arrive. Just as we'd do, they won't make a massive strike in order to avoid hitting their own, but they'll destroy our Goannas quickly. Should I continue?"

"Thank you, Captain Lee. Very good."

"Your permission, Commander, Sir," said Senior Lt. Ivan Ivlev, some five years older than I and who had an engineer troop emblem. He felt a bit awkward in the company of more experienced officers.

"We're listening."

"I keep seeing cadet-commandos fiddling with the quargs' weapons and mastering their robots. I think they're doing it for a reason. I don't know how much we can do, Commander, Sir. For example, I don't understand whether or not we can use the Mammoths and the Large Dragons in the hangars. If so, the picture so vividly described by Captain Lee could change dramatically."

Ivlev was a guy with brains. He was asking the right questions.

"You're thinking along the right lines, Senior Lieutenant. I'm planning on making big use of captured equipment. But it all comes down to one problem. In order to make even one enemy robot obey I need the help of two technicians, a mobile repair kit and at least two hours. If we fight our way to the tech park, we won't even have five minutes. And one heavy robot won't really help us."

"Commander, Sir, if we start with the division commander's robot, then after hacking its defense we could have very wide access to the remote reconfiguration of all the robots in the unit. That's judging by the way such things are organized in our troops. I don't know that much about quarg equipment."

I thought it over. The question had to be studied. I never was concerned before with commanding quarg robots, but such information was available in my tablet.

"This is an interesting idea. I must think it over, but it doesn't solve the problem of two hours, two tech guys and a mobile repair kit. All right, officers and commanders. That's all for now. Go back to your immediate duties."

I continued brainstorming, immersed in the reports of my fellow xenologists who had the pleasure of dissecting captured command quarg robots. I realized that I still remained just a brigadier general, and I won't become a good scientist despite the enormous amount of knowledge at my fingertips. I had missed a few good chances. The quargs differed from humans in their much more centralized approach to everything. I should have drawn useful conclusions from this long ago. A commander is almost like a god for a quarg. A commander's authority over a subordinate is almost absolute.

I knew this, but for some reason my knowledge of it was separate from everything else. Imagine a kind of a spherical horse in a vacuum; in other words, an abstraction, which it turned out, had many implications. For example, from their commander's robot it was possible to change not only the different settings of a subordinate's machine, but also the access codes and even the interaction protocols with other robots. If necessary, a commander could remotely block the control of any robot in his unit. At the same time, a commander couldn't override such control. Apparently, this was technically impossible to do. Communication links were unstable against the background of intense operations by enemy EW stations. Therefore, full remote control was not possible.

That was another brick in the wall of a well-structured plan maturing in my head. But a few holes still needed to be plugged, and the main hole was the time needed to hack an enemy robot. I had 200 years of computer hacking experience in my memory; many hundreds of algorithms that no one on either side of the front here had yet thought of. There were generic vulnerability tables, adaptive security system stability tests, and much more. I had to figure out how to use these many tools, but so far I didn't have any ideas.

I needed to get rid of the need for labor-intensive disassembly and subsequent assembly of the robot. The quargs don't do it when they need to test or run some maintenance. It's not possible to access technical ports from the cockpit, at least with its interface connectors or in a wireless way that's accessible to the pilot. But technicians usually don't go in the cockpit. They work from the outside. A solution came unexpectedly. I called Jeff and asked for a list of captured equipment that we had at our disposal. Fortunately, among the 10 enemy combat space suits was a technician's combat gear. I was already morally prepared to adapt a battle space suit to technical needs, but I didn't have to.

We headed to the senior technician's place. On the way, I explained my idea. Looking into Jeff's glowing eyes, I realized that he also thought we were on the right track. We spent about five hours working on the space suit, and as a result, we got a hacker unit that was protected by armor. It only looked like the quarg tech's suit that it was originally. Before hacking we focused on avoiding the need to fuse the human and quarg interfaces, which were alien to each other. We did this at our base by hacking and modernizing the captured suit. Now using it as an intermediary, we could connect directly to the enemy robots' maintenance ports without disassembling them or getting into the connections deep inside.

The Small Dragon was our guinea pig. I barely was able to get into the captured suit. The difference in anatomy between humans and quargs was a huge issue, and even the suit's ability to adapt to the owner's size didn't help. But I did it. The Small Dragon surrendered in 10 minutes.

Only one final matter remained. Captain Mbia was awake, so I went to him and his men to find out if we could get inside the security perimeter. As it turned out, that was possible. Fortunately, during the retreat the scouts had kept their special equipment, which waited its moment in their fly-car. Mbia warned me, however, that the risk of this was very high. A deafening silence reigned in the room when I presented my plan at the emergency meeting. Finally, Captain Lee smiled sadly.

"I was under the impression that I was listening to a description of a ritual suicide procedure. In particular, of yours first, because you're the one who's going to be the first to go down the dragon's throat and see what it ate tonight. But we all won't outlive you much, and will follow you at that exact moment. After the dragon swallows you it'll realize it's hungry again, and breakfast will have been served. Well, then, so be it."

"You're a romantic, Captain," Mbia answered for me. "I also want to go on living. I have plans, you know. But beyond our concrete barrack walls our comrades await their fate. I'm a Cameroonian. It's not common today to recall national origins, but frankly, I don't give a damn. My great-grandfather used to tell me how our ancestors dealt with their troubles. Now, we're all one tribe because we have a common enemy. With all due respect, Captain Lee, my ancestors wouldn't understand you. In my area of speciality I don't see anything impossible in the commander's plan. That's all I have to say."

"You misunderstood my words, Captain," the Korean responded, smiling. "I only mean that I see a real chance of death and am ready for it. My role in the commander's plan is clear, and I'm sure I can handle it. I can also see that Mr. Lavroff is as ready for death as I am, but he's in no hurry to meet this fate."

I nodded and looked at Minchenko.

"Where will I go? I swore an oath," answered the Captain, shrugging his shoulders. "It may sound okay, theoretically. But let's see what happens in reality."

"I agree with the previous speaker," added Senior Lieutenant Ivlev.

"Commander, Sir," said Inga getting up. "Permission to prepare the battalion for departure."

Chapter 10

We spent two days building up our forces near the target. We used only eight of the 49 dropships that we had re-equipped just like mine. This necessitated the dismantling of all EW stations from the other dropships.

We decided to first move all infantry and robots to a prepared and camouflaged assault line, and then attached the thermobaric rocket launchers from the dropships to our cloaked machines, using them as attack aircraft. The start of the operation's active phase was scheduled for 2 a.m. in order to catch the quargs asleep and with the equipment in the hangars. At the same time, that would still give us enough darkness to make our getaway.

At the appointed time, Mbia with two of his men and myself quietly left the camouflage net, which unfortunately only shielded us from visual detection and ran slightly bending towards the former location of the 2nd Regiment. This part of the operation was the Captain's responsibility. I was here as a sort of passenger and my role was limited to obeying his orders. They told me to run, I ran; they told me to hit the ground, I did it immediately. We waited about three minutes. I didn't see what exactly the captain saw ahead with his sharp scanners.

His men sent forward a dozen, black mechanical 'cockroaches' the size of a well-fed mouse. They cheerfully crawled ahead and disappeared into the night. I didn't interfere with these proven professionals and patiently waited. Soon, the scout who went first signaled to move on, though we now had to crawl. To my shame, I didn't notice when we crossed the security perimeter. I only realized we passed it when I rested on the base's concrete fence.

Here we stayed about 15 minutes: first, we assembled an excavator from the parts that we had brought. It quickly but quietly dug a way under the fence, scanning the ground constantly in front for various surprises and 'gifts' for uninvited guests. Fortunately, none were found. Either they weren't expecting guests, or they didn't have time to work on this; or maybe they simply relied on the security perimeter.

After emerging from the underground passage when inside the base, we looked around carefully. The EW stations in our space suits made us virtually invisible to local enemy scanners on the distance of 30 meters and more. It was strongly advised that no one be allowed nearer than that. According to Mbia, the quargs didn't appear in the yard at night. The area was patrolled by small, specialized security robots moving around the area according to a certain schedule. Sometimes that schedule changed, but not more than once every half hour.

We needed another 15 minutes to cross the courtyard and reach the tech park. The hangar gate was shut with digital locks that the quargs fit into the folds. We thought hacking them was too dangerous, and anyway it wasn't part of the original plan. The tech park building had been built by humans, and Senior Lt. Ivlev knew the location of the back-up and technical entrances, so we took advantage of that. The hatch that blocked access to the cable well appeared to be welded on the outside; it resisted us for just a few minutes. First, we carefully made a small hole with acid and sent recon drones inside the tech park. Seeing that the hatch had no warning devices, we opened it and followed the drones.

There was a deceptive silence in the tech park. Equipment storage areas always had surveillance cameras and multi-band scanners that reacted to anything that moved but only if it was larger than the size specified by the program. We took advantage of that. The black 'cockroaches' were back in business. This time, they were joined by other devices that resembled well-fed 'slugs' and which blended perfectly into the surface of the walls.

They crawled slowly and we had to wait at least half an hour for them to reach their targets, but it was worth the wait. The 'slugs' attached to the walls, releasing next to the cameras and scanners a thin and practically invisible aerosol; while the 'cockroaches' formed a holographic picture with thin lasers that closed the field of view of all the cameras wherever they turned.

The picture reflected everything as it really was, but minus our presence. Something similar happened to the scanners, but there was no clear picture and it seemed the aerosol was of another chemical composition. Since the silence was total, the deception was successful.

It took us a while to find the hangar we needed. The 'cockroaches' crept along a few adjacent rooms and acting together they gave us a record in the form of a circular panorama. Only in the fifth hangar did we find the distinctive silhouette of the commander's Mammoth, which was difficult for us to identify in the image. It stood slightly away from his ordinary companions, as was the standard for the unit commander's machine. It was distinguished by the abundance of additional navigation and communication equipment sensors mounted externally on armor and that formed the machine's unique silhouette.

As the scanners and detectors were deceived one after the other, we slowly and cautiously moved toward our target. Now the roles changed and I was the main actor. My terribly uncomfortable captured space suit finally got a chance to prove itself. Compared to the Small Dragon, the commander's Mammoth was far better protected. My hacker program took almost 30 minutes, but then finally the cabin door was unlocked with a slight click. Silently cursing this quarg contraption that was mistakenly called a space suit, I awkwardly climbed inside.

The second stage of the hacking was more important than the first. Using my command authority I instructed 28 robots of my (now mine!) unit to change the access codes. According to the software report, the replacement was successful. Since I didn't have enough trained pilots for such a group of heavy machines I had to put them on a pilotless march. This is very convenient when you only need to move unit machines from point A to point B. One command machine manned by a human - or a quarg - is enough. The rest follow or go in the right direction even without a commander if they're programmed to march on their own. The latter is not often used, but both we and the enemy have this. In the event of an attack the robots fire on targets designated as hostile by the commander. Any target that opens fire on them automatically gets a hostile status.

Having made sure that my ironmen were ready for battle and marching, I gave the signal to Mbia and his men. They ran to the three nearest Large Dragons. I unlocked access to the cabins, and soon only our 'cockroaches' and 'slugs' remained in the hangar. It was time to start the operation's hot phase. We had wasted more time than planned. Before leaving for the 2nd Regiment base I promised at the right moment to signal to my comrades who waited to attack. I turned the Mammoth towards the hangar gate, and fired the shoulder grenade launcher. This was the signal. The caliber of the grenade launcher didn't leave the gate any chance and blew it wide open. The hangar was hit by a shock wave, sweeping away loose objects, but the Mammoth didn't even budge.

Our plan was to give the quargs a minute to jump out of the ground and out of the concrete buildings. I didn't go outside of the hangar, but instead I took the robot through the incinerated gate and inside since environmental health conditions were going to deteriorate. On my loud signal, eight of our dropships took to the air. Six of them, after having flown a bit towards the former location of the 2nd Regiment, fired simultaneously with all their unguided rockets.

Two other dropships, under the joint command of Captain Lee, set a course for the quarg airbase 30 kilometers west of the main target. They fired rockets two minutes later when the quarg pilots on alert were about to take off to rescue the Heavy Robots Division under attack. In the wake of the dropships' attack our main force - two battalions of commandos and a separate heavy infantry company - burst into the base's security perimeter from the camouflaged line. They were commanded by chief of staff, Captain Minchenko.

We aimed the rockets so that we wouldn't accidentally demolish the barracks and tech park; but the rest of the buildings got the full treatment. All the open space between them turned into a sea of high-intensity flames and raging blast waves that pulverized everything in their path except well-armored or reinforced concrete structures. The hangar roof was blown off instantly. The walls swayed and cracked in some places, but remained standing.

Now, it was our turn to act. The jail break was up to Inga's battalion. Katzman's battalion and Ivlev's heavy infantry had to neutralize the remnants of the quarg combat shields. They were all now busy, and my job was to prevent the enemy from hitting us with a targeted orbital strike and to repulse a possible aerial bombardment following Captain Lee's attack on the airbase.

Instead of the hangar roof, we saw the sky above us with the dots of stars whose light barely penetrated the smoke and dust from the rocket strike. Many of these stars were actually enemy ships, and the largest were in low orbit. They were the biggest threat now, and at top of the list of targets for my robots I gave the order to march, and simultaneously it triggered in their computer brains an automatic mode to follow the commander and fight external threats.

The Mammoths and Large Dragons slightly altered their stances, taking a more stable position. Diaphragm hatches opened in the armored burls on their backs and large surface-to-space missiles burst into the sky. Each robot was carrying two such 'gifts', and now all 28 machines sent 56 missiles to their targets. At such distances their flight time was less than a minute, and in the final stretch of their trajectory the rockets accelerated to almost 12 kilometers per second. Quarg orbital monitors, designed mainly to defend against attacks from outer space, hung above the planet, with their vulnerable side turned towards it.

The semi-spheres, 300 meters in diameter, had thick armor, powerful main-caliber cannons and multiple missile defenses on the bow facing any potential enemy. The flat stern had much weaker armor and with a propulsion system that was poorly protected because of its design features. Needless to say, a sudden stab in the back from the planet that the quargs seemed to be in complete control of came as a very unpleasant surprise. These 22 monitors controlled the space above us. The rest were hanging too far to be able to significantly impact the course of the battle. Thus, there were two to three missiles per target. It was not possible to destroy the 300-

meter armored monster with two or three hits. But to damage and immobilize it, and to put it out of play for a while, that just might be possible with help from our missiles.

The loading machines rolled to the robots that just fired and started to quickly load missiles into their knapsack launchers. While they were doing that, I took my Mammoth out of the tech park. The bright flares in the sky above signaled that the missiles had hit their targets. One of the flashes was larger and brighter than the others. It looked like one of the orbital monitors was fatally unlucky. We should have left the former 2nd Regiment base as soon as possible.

The scanner made an unpleasant squeal, and a few shells hit my robot. The caliber was insufficient to penetrate the Mammoth's armor, but I got the signal that the quargs who survived the rocket strike were returning to their senses. I fired three grenades in the direction from which I was fired upon, and then jumped past the concrete corner of the barracks. A Goanna ran past me, firing incessantly with a rotary machine gun. A squad of commandos rushed after it. I wasn't distracted by enemy infantry and led the reloaded division away from the base.

"Commander," Inga called me on the radio. "The barracks are under our control. Our prisoners are fine. The quargs surrendered there. What to do with them?"

"I take it there are no dead or wounded among our prisoners? The quargs didn't try to shoot them?"

"That's right. They didn't."

"Then tell the quargs to take off all their combat gear and lock them up somewhere in a store room. They don't deserve to die today, but we can't take them with us."

"Are you sure, Commander, Sir?" Captain Minchenko interjected into our conversation. "In a battle, all enemies are destroyed."

"I'm sure, Captain; as sure as I'll ever be. They didn't hurt our prisoners even though they could have shot half, maybe all of them. Mercy must be encouraged. Today we won't kill them, tomorrow they won't shoot our guys. Do it."

I acted on the experience of my past life. The war against the toads was waged with cruelty and ruthlessness. But there were unwritten rules. Neither we nor the toads ever burned a city with a civilian population, unless they offered resistance. In fact, genocide was not practiced, although, there were exceptions. Prisoner exchanges became common. In 100 years of war, this procedure had been polished to perfection. Sometimes asymmetrical exchanges happened. Once, in order to be allowed to evacuate the inhabitants of a populous planet that we had captured, the toads left the strategically important star system without fighting. But this was not always the case. At the beginning of the war, no one took prisoners or spared enemy cities. And then someone, no one remembers who, at the right moment gave the order not to shoot.

The POWs were loaded into the dropships, of which only seven remained. One didn't return from the attack on the enemy airbase. Captain Lee, to my great regret, was correct in his premonition that the coming battle would be his last.

"Enemy resistance has been neutralized," reported Ivlev. "We have nine dead and six wounded. No serious injuries."

"Clear, Senior Lieutenant. Katzman, report," I called to the 2nd battalion commander.

"Bringing the battalion to the muster point: 15 killed, nine wounded, three seriously. The enemy destroyed four Goannas."

"Immediately load the wounded into the dropships and send them to the base together with the former POWs."

I knew the quargs wouldn't let us go quietly. Launching missiles into the enemy's orbital group was able to disrupt them for a while, but soon they'll bring in ships from high orbit and send in aircraft from distant bases.

As if to support of my words, the three Large Dragons turned northwest and fired six ground-to-air missiles at unseen targets. It was a hint that we shouldn't linger.

I took my robots outside the base fence and divided them into two unequal groups. Eighteen robots led by my Mammoth marched quickly towards the canyon system where we first met Captain Mbia. We were joined by Inga's battalion and Ivlev's heavy infantry. In the canyons we'd already set up shelters that were cloaked by camouflage and covered by EW stations. We were supposed to remain there while our modernized dropships took the freed POWs back to the base and then returned for us.

A second group of 10 Mammoths and Large Dragons, along with Israel Katzman's battalion, moved in the opposite direction. Unlike us, their task was to deflect the quarg wrath. I'd written off the heavy robots moving in an autonomous march as losses in advance. As far as Katzman's people, we set up a small camouflaged shelter about halfway to where they should have gone. The remaining battalion Goannas had to be sacrificed for the sake of authenticity. It was important to make the picture of our column's defeat as realistic as possible.

The first point on the route of the diversion group was the quarg airbase. Heavy robots fired missiles at it from about 15 kilometers. A drone scout sent to the base after the strike found that at least half the missiles hit their targets. In fact, after two strikes, first by rockets from the dropships and then by fire from the robots, the base ceased to exist. Not a single atmospheric aircraft was able to take off.

The quargs, of course, weren't going to tolerate this. Battleships in low orbit fired approximately 50 rockets in a demonstrative column. At the same time, enemy aircraft came to the battlefield from three directions. Destroying even one heavy robot is not easy. In addition to firing missiles, it can also shoot them down.

By the time of the attack, Katzman's battalion had left the column, which was going along the route and fighting in automatic mode. Fifteen Goannas fired at enemy aircraft with missiles from their knapsack launchers but their salvos got lost in a sea of fire that the Mammoths and Large Dragons unleashed on the quargs. In the 'hand' of each heavy robot was a rotary machine gun, much larger than the one that the Goannas had. Their knapsack launchers contained not only heavy missiles capable of reaching into space, but also smaller caliber and range ammo. The quargs' atmospheric ships were washed with their blood, with more than half of the machines gone, but first they were able to fire their missiles.

Stopping for a few seconds, the heavy robots fired surface-to-space missiles at enemy ships in low orbit. A veritable hell burst forth in the combat order of the demonstrative column. Still, the firing density of the quargs, who were furious at our daring raid, exceeded all reasonable limits. Even 10 heavy robots were unable to shoot down all the missiles that targeted them. You don't even have to mention the Goannas. The heavy missiles fired from the battleships tore the Mammoths and Dragons apart, but not many of these rockets reached the robots because they were priority targets for the column's anti-air defense. When an aerial missile hit a Goanna this light robot had no chance, but his heavy brethren could take a hit, although it would sustain damage.

When the tornado of fire raging over the column subsided, only three machines continued to move along the planned route. The Mammoths were better protected, and they survived. Two robots totally lost their manipulators that replaced their arms; all three machines were left without hinged equipment and their scanners were virtually blind.

Driven by a relentless program, the Mammoths marched forward, continuing to shoot as enemy targets fell into their guidance systems' reduced field of view. These robots were finished off from orbit. They had almost nothing left to shoot down a heavy missile, and this once formidable force of 10-meter giants were now scattered about as smoking debris amid explosions. But they had done their job: our main force reached the shelters without further casualties.

***

The regiment assembled in full only a week later. We were reluctant to reveal our base location, and with great care the upgraded dropships transported equipment and people from temporary shelters at night. Only on the third day were we able to start because quarg aircraft had literally been flying over our heads constantly.

We had to fake our base in a maze of ravines, where the remnants of the defeated 105th tried to retreat some time ago. To do that, we took a launcher from one of the Large Dragons and two tons of various ammo. As night fell, two surface-to-space missiles were launched from the ravine. They were, of course, easily shot down and answered with fire. Apparently, the massive explosion that followed the first hit by a quarg rocket convinced them that they had destroyed something important. While it didn't happen immediately, their activity in the sky above us returned to a normal level.

When Captain Mbia's scouts and I were among the last to return to the base, our camp was droning and buzzing like a beehive in an anthill, with people running around. Having been so determined to help people escape the quarg backlash, I had overlooked the fact that the former

POWs arrived at the base first, and for a while they were on their own. They were given rations, but the immediate focus shifted to caring for the wounded. Considering our situation, this proved to be a non-trivial task. Fortunately, among the freed were medical personnel, and so this problem was more or less solved. I guess that's why they didn't bother me, except with a brief report that all the necessary assistance had been provided.

We freed almost 150 POWs, and along with the wounded commandos and infantry they barely fit in our seven dropships. Among the freed were 12 officers, three of whom were majors, one lieutenant colonel, and most interestingly, we freed Colonel Cooper, commander of the 2nd Regiment of the 105th.

And then the Colonel started to become active.

Inga ran up to me, speaking in a manner not sanctioned by army regulations.

"Igor, Colonel Cooper rounded up the officers of the 2nd Regiment, took over your headquarters, and suspended your commanding officers. He claimed that as a senior officer he is in charge. Doesn't want to hear about you at all. The Lt. Colonel and majors listen to him, although only two are from the 2nd Regiment. There was nothing anyone could do because they're high-ranking officers."

I thought it over. A conflict between our officers was the last thing I needed now. But I was not going to hand over control of the regiment to the officer who failed in battle, even though it had been unequal, and then surrendered. Mbia, who also exited the dropship, heard Inga very well. I turned to him.

"What would you say, Captain?"

"What can I say, Commander? Scouts! Take your weapons!"

We walked under the cave vaults, and from the back, right and left of the aisles armored soldiers appeared. Our procession was joined by combat robots. With iron banging and servers humming our company went to the doors of HQ. A guard in armor tried to block my way, but Captain Mbia's scout, who appeared from the side, instantly neutralized him, and carefully put him on the ground with his armored suit without injuring the soldier. I opened the door carefully and took a step inside, ordering my men with a gesture to stay outside.

"At your command, officers, Sirs," I said, putting my hand on the battle helmet visor. "To what do I owe the pleasure of your visit to my headquarters? I don't remember inviting you."

There were five officers. Those same three majors, a lieutenant colonel and the commander of the 2nd Regiment, Colonel Cooper.

"You're out of line, Cadet!" The Colonel jumped up from behind my desk. "Leave HQ immediately. There's a command meeting going on and cadets don't belong here. Major Bronski, have security show him out!"

A short major closest to the exit bolted out the door, but urgently returned with a perplexed look on his face.

"That's you, Colonel, Sir, who is out of line here," I responded icily. "You forgot three things. First, it was my unit that freed you from captivity. According to the unwritten laws of war a soldier or officer of any rank, upon release from captivity, must submit to the unit commander that freed him until the operation ends."

This was in fact my improvisation. There were no such rules here, but this was so in my last life and I wasn't gonna give them up. "Second, I was assigned to command the landing regiment by direct order of Admiral Petrov who led the planet's orbital defense until his heroic demise. Here, officers, Sirs, kindly familiarize yourself with the order," and I sent them the file. "Third, I'm the only one here who can ensure combat cohesion and control of a unit in which half of the equipment has been captured from the enemy."

There was silence. The officers were reading the Admiral's order, but the Colonel was not yet ready to admit defeat.

"The Admiral appointed you, Cadet, to command a training regiment struggling to stay alive in a critical situation and in the complete absence of officers. Yes, it authorizes you to add to your unit disparate and disorganized groups of soldiers and officers who lost their units. But you have no authority to take command of regular units, stationed on the planet and headed by the officers in charge."

This argument was getting on my nerves. But I decided to be patient.

"Colonel, Sir, where do you see a regular unit? In quarg captivity? Or perhaps in the area of your regiment captured by the enemy? The fact that you and a few of your staff officers managed to survive doesn't make your regiment an organized unit. I can simply arrest you, Colonel, Sir, for sabotage and attempted riot, but I won't do that. If you have the will, take your men and leave our base. I'll provide arms and supplies since we recovered enough from your regiment's former location. Go and show the quargs how regular Earth Federation army units fight!

The Colonel started to cave in. Everyone present felt it. He frowned at me and after a brief pause, he said: "I'll relent in the face of pressure, Cadet. Now isn't the time to have a fight. But the time will come. In the meantime, we have to survive and wait for our fleet. I'm ready to submit to you, Cadet, but I demand to keep the 2nd Regiment of the 105th as a separate subdivision in your unit."

"No, Colonel, Sir," that insects like this should be pressed to the max is something I learned in my past life. "Either you join my regiment unconditionally, or my men will remove you as soon as you get your weapons and equipment. Decide. You have five minutes," I turned and left HQ, carefully closing the door.

When I returned, five officers came up to meet me.

"Commander, Sir," Colonel Cooper spoke in a grim, hard voice. "The 2nd Regiment of the 105th Infantry is at your disposal. Waiting for your orders."

Chapter 11

The battle in high orbit above Leiten-5 reached its logical conclusion. Federation ships pressed the quargs down to the planet; they already knocked out all their line forces and were finishing off the rest of the loose change. The result was entirely to be expected. The Admiralty didn't hesitate and sent in the entire 5th Strike Fleet. The insolent quarg foray demanded an exemplary response.

Colonel-General Knyazev, commander of the fleet's commando corps, ordered the landing craft to move to the planet. A bloody battle was imminent there. The quargs clearly wanted to hold on to the planet at all costs, but they didn't have time to build a full-scale orbital defense and had limited themselves to a network of monitors and mobile cover forces. They didn't spare any money on building up ground forces, as well as their anti-space and anti-air defense systems.

"Colonel-General, Sir, Fleet Admiral Nelson is on the line."

Knyazev nodded and turned to the projection screen from which looked the man with the legendary naval commander's namesake.

"Pavel," Nelson, who was in high spirits, informally addressed the General. "Tell me where to punch holes. Where do you plan to land?"

"Orbital recon data is not yet complete," Knyazev answered. "We have to get closer and scan the surface more carefully."

"Colonel-General, Sir!" the voice of the space control operator interrupted their dialogue. "Surface-to-space missiles have been launched from the planet."

"Have they gone mad down there?" The general was surprised. "There's nothing in low orbit except their own monitors and some tiny ships hiding behind them."

"Pavel, the quargs are taking action," responded Nelson, who was still on the line. "They're trying to shoot down these missiles! Do we have troops left on the planet that can reach low orbit? Why don't we know about this?"

"Two infantry divisions were stationed on the planet. The 102nd and 105th. According to the latest data from the planet, they were defeated by the quargs and ceased organized resistance…"

"Some quarg orbital monitors are hit," reported the operator. "Two monitors destroyed, five damaged and immobilized. I'm watching a battle on the planet surface;" the battle area was marked with red shading on a tactical hologram.

"Admiral, we're being invited down, don't you think?"

"We? No, Colonel-General. Not we, but rather, you're invited. I won't go. That's not my business – to dive into the atmosphere. You – you're clearly invited."

"Well, Fleet Admiral, Sir, here's the answer to your question - where to punch a hole. Somebody already started doing it for you. Join them."

"Received," replied Nelson and cut off.

"So, analysts. Info. Quick: Who could it be? Who else was on the planet at the time of the quarg attack?"

"Colonel-General…"

"Forget the formalities."

"Several other small units there were trained in combat cohesion, but they only had light weapons. It's obviously not them…"

"Who else?"

"Just a second…. There's information that at the moment of the quarg attack the transport ship *Macedonia,* escorted by the corvette *Impetuous-1415,* came out of hyperspace. A cadet regiment of the Planetary Commando Academy arrived on Leiten-5 to train in landing. They emerged in the thick of the battle. The corvette was immediately destroyed and the transport ship seriously damaged, and then drifted uncontrollably towards the planet. It was soon finished off, but the commandos escaped and entered the atmosphere. There's no more information."

"A training commando regiment…" repeated the General wistfully. "It doesn't add up. They've nothing heavier than Goannas; plus unguided thermobaric rocket systems in dropships. But here someone is reaching low orbit from the surface…"

Enemy monitor marks on the tactical hologram were disappearing one by one.

"The expected time to open a safe passage through the orbital defense is 14 minutes," reported the tactical operator.

"I need scanner data, as detailed as possible. Use a spyglass if you like, but I need to know who's fighting on the planet. Did you try to get in touch with them?"

"Yes, Sir. Quargs are jamming all bands."

"When will we get data from the surface?"

"We got to get closer. In 10-12 minutes."

The General squeezed the arms of his chair. He understood what was happening on the surface: some kind of unit managed to hide out in a safe haven during the quarg occupation of the planet, and now when the Federation fleet has arrived, they put it all on the line and struck at enemy ground forces and, above all, at their anti-aircraft and anti-space defenses, trying to seize and keep a foothold for the commando landing. If they have enough strength to do what they plan, they'll save at least a full commando division for the Federation.

If they do not have the strength to fight and they fail, and the quargs destroy them before help from orbit arrives, then the quargs will meet this help with a salvo from all their cannons and casualties will probably be greater than if the commandos hadn't been in a hurry and landed with massive support from orbit. A decision had to be taken right now. For a handful of people fighting on the surface of Leiten-5 every minute might be the last.

Minutes passed, the planet was closer and the battle on the surface continued.

"We've got the scanner data… There's an image from the surface… But, Colonel-General, Sir, that's not possible."

"Show the image on the screen, quickly."

On the screen appeared a 3D image taken from above. The quality was very poor. Smoke and dust from explosions interfered with one's normal perception, but computer filtration soon cleared the image of interference, supplemented with data from multi-band scanners. The image finally became clear.

On the rocky surface moving in joint formation and firing without interruption, it was possible to see Goannas, which the General was used to seeing. But totally alien in this context were the heavy quarg robots that stood 10 meters tall. Light Small Dragons were also seen in two places. Now it was clear who was shooting at the enemy's monitors, but many questions remained.

"What's happening there? Analysts, answer quickly! Or I'll put you in a dropship and you'll be in the first landing wave!"

"Five more seconds... Here! Definitely commandos from the *Macedonia*. Shortly before the quarg attack their Academy board approved a new course on mastering captured equipment. They've got a top-notch expert on this matter. I mean, it's a bit far-fetched, but..."

"It could pass for a theory. Now let's assess the situation. Can they hold the corridor for us?"

The image of the battle on the screen and the tactical hologram looked frightening. Waves of enemy aircraft were rolling onto a slowly expanding foothold. The enemy ground forces, which were only 10 minutes behind the air force, were approaching, and they had already opened fire with long-range missiles. Eighteen heavy robots met the enemy with a barrage of fire. So far, they have managed, with the help of the Goannas and Small Dragons, to shoot down almost all the missiles heading towards them.

At the same time, the Mammoths and the Dragons answered the quarg aircraft, but the amount of ammo used in this mode of combat was excessive. The loading machines followed the robots' combat order, and it was something out of the nightmare of any professor of tactics. General Knyazev understood the reason for such a violation of official instructions: the air defense umbrella would collapse without immediate ammo resupply, as would the entire operation.

"The battle analysis software calculates that they won't last long. It draws attention to gross violations of tactical recommendations and predicts the unit's effectiveness at 60% of its maximum capability."

"That's ridiculous. They're fighting very well. Quickly do a retrospective analysis of the last five minutes of combat with computer prediction and real performance."

"Done. Computer forecast - the same 60 percent. In fact..." the analyst fell silent.

"What?! Do I have to beat it out of you?"

"132 percent."

"Transport ships, engines at full power. Landing modules be ready to discharge the dropships. Contact Fleet Admiral Nelson. Now!"

"Contact established."

"Admiral, I need orbital support now. Look what's happening on the surface."

"But my analysts claim..."

"Nelson, they're talking nonsense together with our computers. They estimate the effectiveness of the battle to be half that of the actual. I checked it."

"But how…"

"As you like, Admiral! I! Need! Support! From orbit! Nelson, those guys down there are dying right now, saving the lives of tens of thousands of our guys. Help them. You know me, I'm not just gonna ask. It's my responsibility."

"I know you, General. I know you very well," Nelson answered with a predatory smile and cut off.

"Drop point!" the tactical operator reported.

"Send the first wave!" ordered Knyazev, and he put the landing operation in an irreversible phase.

"Drop done!"

The tactical hologram bloomed with hundreds of red dropships dots rushing to the planet through the penetrated corridor. No shots were fired, although the first casualties were expected by that time, according to the operation plan.

"Prepare to land the heavy weapons regiment."

"Colonel-General, Sir, it's too risky…" the senior analyst had the courage to confront the commander.

"Nothing of the sort. The real first wave is already on the surface. We've just sent a second one, even though it's the first for us. Now it's time for heavy weapons. They go at the same time as our second wave. That's it! End of discussion. Do it!"

"Yes, Sir!"

The battle for the foothold continued to be displayed on the projection screen. The defenders initially numbered 18 Mammoths and Large Dragons. Now, 10 remained. The boundaries of the bridgehead began to tighten slowly. The rows of Goannas and Small Dragons also had gaping holes, and the whole bridgehead was lit with debris and burning machinery. The loading machines were almost all gone, and the foothold defenders were almost out of ammo. But there was a new factor to be considered in the battle.

Numerous guided bombs and missile warheads from heavy ships that broke through to low orbit began to explode among the enemy robots and infantry units attacking the foothold. This cost our fleet four badly damaged cruisers, but Nelson kept his promise. The pressure on the foothold dropped sharply. At the moment when the loading machine of the Commander's Mammoth dry-clicked, indicating ammo depletion, Colonel-General Knyazev's dropships were already landing on the ground behind the heavy robot's back.

For a while, the bridgehead defenders supported the incoming wave of troops with fire, but gradually they were forced out of the battle as their ammo ended. Knyazev's people, however, managed to finish the job. They avoided the bloodiest part of the landing - the capture of the bridgehead. Then the commandos on the ground had to expand the area and to ensure the safe landing of major ships with regular infantry. And it wasn't their first time doing this.

"I want to see the commander and the senior officers of this unit," said the now calm Colonel-General. "Get them out of there. They've done their job."

***

A small transport ship, a little larger than my usual Cuirassier, brought us into orbit. General Knyazev ordered the regimental leadership to join him personally. I insisted on evacuating the wounded, stating that none of the officers would leave our base until it was done, which was why we were now on our way to General Knyazev's flagship with our infirmary.

Despite the presence of three majors, a lieutenant colonel and a colonel in my regiment, I decided to leave the tried and tested commanders in their places. Of the freed POWs I selected combat robot pilots, and after testing their abilities and skills I entrusted them with 18 Goannas whose pilots moved into the captured heavy machines. Of the remaining infantrymen I formed another company that I named the 2nd infantry regiment out of respect for the colonel, and put Cooper in charge, giving him all the new officers. The result was a cumbersome and bizarre structure, but that was historically the case.

My consolidated regiment now consisted of two commando battalions under the command of Katzman and Inga; Captain Mbia's scouts company; the separate heavy infantry company of Senior Lt. Ivlev; the second infantry regiment of Cooper; and our primary strike force - the heavy robots' division - the command of which I left for myself. We also had to have a medical unit with a hospital. In this formation, apart from the medical unit, we had struck at the quarg defenses.

In preparation to face our superiors, I brought Captain Minchenko, chief of staff, and Colonel Cooper as the senior officer of the consolidated regiment. I didn't expect much trouble from him. After our conflict he somehow pulled himself together, put his ambition in its proper place, or maybe, hopefully, by some miracle, he figured it out and learned something. In any case, during our attack and in the subsequent defense of the bridgehead he was not afraid and guided his soldiers quite competently.

In the flagship's hangar we were met by a senior lieutenant in an impeccable uniform who looked suspiciously at my cadet's shoulder straps.

"Colonel, Sir, the Commander is waiting for you," he told Cooper.

"Lead, Senior Lieutenant.," nodded the Colonel.

"May I ask, Colonel, is the cadet coming with you?" the lieutenant asked, casting a glance at me.

Cooper hemmed and suddenly answered: "Yeah, it's more like we're going with the cadet than he's going with us."

The Senior Lieutenant was perplexed and decided not to ask any more questions. Let the brass deal with this weirdness on their own.

We were stopped before entering the flagship command post, and the captain in charge of the guards on duty also took an interest in my humble person. He asked if the cadet could wait outside, or if the colonel really saw the need for him to be present at the meeting with the Commander. The Colonel saw the need and the Captain didn't argue.

We entered the command post and stopped to report. Upon seeing our mixed company, which was rather colorful due to the presence of a first-year cadet, General-Colonel Knyazev raised his eyebrow slightly, but took his time with the questions, waiting for us to introduce ourselves.

"Colonel-General, Sir…" as the senior officer among us Cooper started the report, "…the commanding officers of the Consolidated Commando Regiment of the Planetary Commando Academy reporting as ordered. Commander of the 2nd Infantry Regiment of the 105th Division, which provisionally belongs to the Consolidated Commando Regiment, Colonel Cooper."

The General's eyebrow rose a few millimeters, showing increased confusion.

"I don't quite understand," said the General. "You, Colonel, command a part of the combined regiment, but are not its commander. That's quite interesting. Introduce your comrades."

"Captain Minchenko," Cooper introduced the next highest ranking officer in our company. "Chief of Staff of the Consolidated Commando Regiment."

The flagship command post plunged into an uneasy silence, and taking advantage of the pause Colonel Cooper continued, turning to me.

"Cadet-Instructor Lavroff. Commander of the United Commando Regiment."

I stood at attention and put my hand on the cap visor.

"I didn't understand," said the rather perplexed General. "Cadet, did you really lead the fight? I have no complaints about the regiment's actions; quite the opposite. But how did you end up commanding a unit worthy to be called the Heavy Commando Brigade?"

I had to recall and show Admiral Petrov's orders. I didn't mention our conflict with the Colonel in the report. Cooper, who was clearly nervous, became calm.

"Oh... I've seen a lot of things during my service, but nothing like that..." the Colonel-General said thoughtfully. "Here, ehh, Lavroff, I don't even know what to call you. Arrange for your men to board the flagship. Thanks for a job well done. Regiment personnel will get three days of rest. I'm waiting for your list of fighters and commanders who distinguished themselves in battle. They'll get state awards. We'll decide what to do with your unit after the landing operation is over. In the meantime, Sir, Commander of the Combined Heavy Brigade of the Planetary Commandos, I confirm your authority until further notice. You deserved it."

I felt a sense of déjà vu. Yes, now I was a cadet, but I'd already been a brigadier general, and it wasn't a dream. Even for a few days I was again in command of a brigade. Fate has a sense of humor, though sometimes rather grim.

***

Our brigade was decommissioned, and I didn't expect anything else. The soldiers and officers were sent to their units or to newly-formed fighting forces. I was told that a new transport ship assigned to the Academy in place of the deceased *Macedonia* was sent for us. But we got a lot of nice things; really. I was not excessively modest when I gave General Knyazev the award lists. Having in mind a loss report of 30 percent of what was expected, he treated my lists with total understanding. Almost half of the names of soldiers and officers presented with awards were marked "posthumously", which greatly darkened the joy of victory.

Israel Katzman perished. He commanded his battalion until the very end from the cockpit of his Goanna, which was half-destroyed by an enemy shell. Captain Ivlev and Cadet Stephen Fulton were seriously injured. Chen, a friend of Stephen, died when along with his platoon he tried to close a breach in the foothold's defense perimeter. Another 200 names of soldiers and cadets, not all of which I knew personally, were on the list of dead and seriously injured. That was the sad arithmetic of war, but their sacrifice saved more than 10,000 lives. That's also arithmetic, but the numbers are with the opposite sign.

Our qualification levels were recalculated; but not for everyone at once. Apparently, processing and reconciling battle reports takes time, but on the third day of our stay on board the flagship the appearance of first-year cadets left junior officers and seasoned commandos in a state of paralysis.

A qualification tab was a curious invention of the local military. In my previous life, nothing like this was ever practiced. Apparently, 20 years of war taught these humans that a commander should be able to see immediately, without reports or questions, who he is dealing with: an experienced veteran, or a green military school graduate. The tab reflected combat experience and theoretical training. There were three categories of combat experience: on the level of a soldier and/or a sergeant; an officer's experience; and senior command positions in battle.

Successful operations increased each soldier's combat experience according to their role in battle. Defeats and mistakes could easily reduce it. Qualifying points took into account a situation's complexity, the relative strength of the parties and many other parameters, each of which increased or decreased the amount of experience points by means of appropriate coefficients. An officer could only gain the next rank by obtaining the needed combat experience and having the necessary theoretical training.

It was a very convenient system. Incompetent commanders simply did not move up in ranks.

Our regiment's plight on Leiten-5 was dire: not just difficult, but almost hopeless. It was just enough to imagine the balance of power between the sides, and the tripling of experience immediately didn't seem excessive. And this was just one of the coefficients. What about the action in the enemy's rear, on an occupied planet? One tripling more. The battle efficiency of over 130 percent calculated by the ship's computers? Creating a formation from the remnants of the defeated and uncontrolled units? And combat operations that were very highly atypical?

After all, while we were not trained as saboteurs, we were intensively engaged in sabotage and guerrilla activities. Our cadets looked like epic heroes, even compared to experienced warriors who had fought for several years but didn't face such extreme conditions. That was quite normal. The regular commandos were well aware of this situation and understood to whom one in three of them owed his life. The guys saluted us when we met in the halls of the flagship.

When I looked at Inga's qualification tab, I just shook my head in admiration. Commanding a platoon and then a battalion in such an operation is truly a great experience. Had it not been for her young age and lack of higher military education, she could have been promoted to the rank of captain and given a battalion. But now that the tension of combat was gone I suddenly realized how long it had been since Inga and I were together. Not on the job, but just like that, for no apparent reason. I also felt that my attention was somehow shifting smoothly from her breast tab to what was underneath. Inga smiled and having taken my hand, pulled me to her cabin. She understands my mood so well.

***

I was the last to get my qualification tab. General Knyazev did it himself. This time the commander spoke to me alone and ordered to report to his office.

"Now, Cadet Lavroff," said the General after listening to my report and ordering me to sit in the visitor's chair. "You've done a lot; many good things actually. Honestly, I want a commander like you in my corps. What do you say?"

"I'm honored, Colonel-General, Sir," I answered, a little puzzled. "But how do you see that?"

"I can't for the time being," Knyazev grinned. "You're 16 years old, and the rank of officer is not given before 18. You got four university diplomas. It's really amazing. But they're all civilian, and you can't become an officer without a higher military education. Unless the Federation

President decides otherwise by his personal order. But I don't think it's possible," said Knyazev, grinning again. "You still have two and a half years left at the Academy; so while we'll be apart, we'll stay in touch. I'll write a review to your Academy director regarding your 'exercises'. I think he'll pass you. I'll send my personal contact info on your tablet. If you need anything, get in touch. I won't forget to whom my guys owe their lives."

Knyazev took a short break and looked at me cunningly. I waited in silence.

"Speaking of the President, in about six months you'll go to the capital and meet him. I recommended you for the Gold Star. Admiral Nelson approved the honor, and the President always presents the Federation's highest award in person."

I got up and replied according the regulations: "Serving…

"Sit down, Lavroff, that's not all," the General waved his hand and took my new qualification tab, along with two small boxes, out of the drawer. "That's yours. You deserved it."

Epilogue

I can't say that our return to the Academy was a triumph because many were not with us, having lost their lives in battle. Nevertheless, we were honored by the welcoming speech of Lt. General Schiller whose hair had become much more gray. There was even a solemn parade in front of the Academy with all our battered equipment, including a Mammoth and a Large Dragon that I obtained for the Academy by asking General Knyazev. He didn't mind.

A week later, I was called to the Lt. General's office. He listened to my report, nodded and pointed for me to sit in a chair at the conference table.

"Cadet Lavroff, yesterday I was contacted by Colonel-General Knyazev. You made a very favorable impression on him and I'm sure you deserved it. He asked me to arrange a personalized training program for you. Our Academy has never done this before, but then we never before had cadets with Expert and Unique specialist badges, and even one recommended for the Gold Star."

The General fell silent and checked something on his tablet.

"Your qualification tab, Lavroff, impressed even me, and I've seen a lot, believe me. But you can't become an officer with a tab like this. While you have more than enough combat experience, it's all in command positions - officer and even senior command positions. You don't have any experience on the level of a soldier or a sergeant. You can't become an officer without it. You should know what a soldier feels and how he acts in battle. You have to figure that out the hard way."

I was waiting silently for the continuation.

"The Academy will send you to do individual practice. Appreciate it, Cadet, this is the first time in the history of the Academy."

"Serving…"

"No need; you're not in line. In three days you fly to the Kapteen star system. It's in the middle of nowhere. One of its planets has oxygen, though few natural resources. We had a colony there but it was unsustainable and we evacuated it. Then the quargs appeared and there's been a low-intensity fight there for about five years. Neither we nor the quargs need the planet, but neither wants to leave it to the enemy. It's a great place to get combat experience as an enlisted soldier, though you don't need much of that. Our infantry division and special forces battalion are deployed there. My old pal, Colonel Kreps, serves there, and he owes me a favor," said the General grinning. "He'll take you in, Cadet, and arrange everything. Any questions?"

"General, Sir, am I going to work with special forces?"

"The Colonel will decide that on the spot, but most likely, yes, and possibly as a universal commando."

"Then, may I prepare my equipment using Academy Tech Zone facilities?"

"Get used to it, Lavroff. Now you're an Expert and Unique specialist. You can do a lot that others can't. You can choose your weapons and equipment. That's quite rare for a cadet."

***

Unlike the journey to Leiten-5, the flight to the Kapteen star system was without incident. Our fleet was firmly in control of the planet's northern hemisphere, while the quargs dominated the southern hemisphere. Skirmishes occurred, but the orbital fortresses didn't allow any activity on the other's territory.

Colonel Kreps received me well, scratched the back of his head while reading my personnel file. He looked with interest at my badges and tab, and contacted the Commander of the Special Forces Battalion, Major Weber. I was given a fly-car and then the Colonel told me the destination, surname and rank of my future immediate superior, and ordered me to head for the battalion.

***

I landed the fly-car on the tarmac of the base of the special forces battalion. After having spent time in the cool, air-conditioned cabin, the heat outside weighed down on me as a physically tangible press. The desert's proximity was felt. Nearby, technicians prepared the dropship for flight. I asked where I could find Lt. Alexey Egorov. One of the guys stopped his work, took a quick look at my cadet uniform, and waved me in the right direction.

I found Egorov coming out of the headquarters building. He looked both angry and thoughtful and concerned about some issue. I caught up with my new commander and called out to him:

"Lieutenant, Sir, may I address to you?"

To be continued.
Brigadier General. Book 2 . Fire Density.

Made in the USA
Las Vegas, NV
01 August 2021